"I have read the first Emily Sparkes book and I really LOVE it . . . it's lots [...........................] thy Cassidy, bestselling au[..................................] series

"Utterly hilarious and [..................................] just gets all of the awful p[..................] eleven years old. Everything in Emily Sparkes's life is a crisis, and each crisis is funnier than the last. Bring on the next book!"
Robin Stevens, author of *Murder Most Unladylike*
(Wells and Wong Mysteries)

"I laughed and laughed at *Emily Sparkes and the Friendship Fiasco*! She's like a younger Georgia Nicolson."
Susie Day, author of *Pea's Book of Best Friends*
(Pea's Book series)

"Lots to appeal to fans of Cathy Cassidy and Dork Diaries in this funny new series" *Bookseller*

"Once you start reading this book you won't be able to put it down. It's true to life and very funny. Emily Sparkes is everyone's dream best friend!" Alice, 12

"I thought this was side-splittingly funny and very realistic. Emily Sparkes is someone I'd want to be friends with!" Sterrett, 10

"Emily Sparkes is my new favourite character. She made me laugh a lot!" Piper, 11

"Emily Sparkes is amazingly funny." Maddie, 12

For more fab reviews visit www.ruthfitzgerald.co.uk

By Ruth Fitzgerald

Emily Sparkes and the Friendship Fiasco
Emily Sparkes and the Competition Calamity
Emily Sparkes and the Disco Disaster
Emily Sparkes and the Backstage Blunder

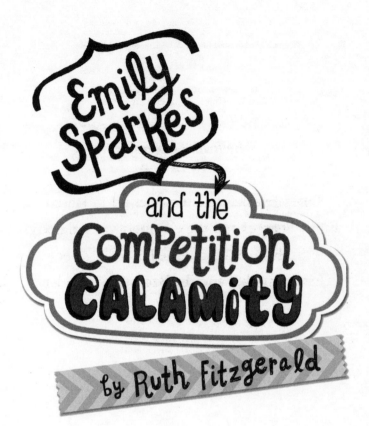

Emily Sparkes and the Competition Calamity

by Ruth Fitzgerald

LITTLE, BROWN BOOKS FOR YOUNG READERS
www.lbkids.co.uk

LITTLE, BROWN BOOKS FOR YOUNG READERS

First published in Great Britain in 2015 by Hodder & Stoughton

1 3 5 7 9 10 8 6 4 2

Text copyright © 2015 by Ruth Fitzgerald
Illustrations copyright © 2015 by Allison Cole

The moral rights of the author and illustrator have been asserted.

A CIP catalogue record for this book
is available from the British Library.

ISBN 978-0-349-00184-5

Typeset in Minion by M Rules
Printed and bound in Great Britain by
Clays Ltd, St Ives plc

The paper and board used in this book are made
from wood from responsible sources.

MIX
Paper from
responsible sources
FSC® C104740

Little, Brown Books for Young Readers,
An imprint of Hachette Children's Group
Part of Hodder & Stoughton
Carmelite House
50 Victoria Embankment
London EC4Y 0DZ

An Hachette UK Company
www.hachette.co.uk

www.hachettechildrens.co.uk

CONTENTS

To Louis, sorry about the Easter egg.

CHAPTER ONE

For Goodness' Sake,
Not Another Pasta Bake

Sunday

My Perfect Mother

*My mum is so fantastic, she makes
cakes and cleans and cooks,
She does the washing and the
ironing and cares about her
looks.*

She wears such lovely dresses and
arranges pretty flowers,
    She helps me with my homework or sits
and sews for hours.
    Her hair is soft and shiny, it's pretty
and it's curled,
    She bakes me cookies after
school, yes, she is the best mum
in the world.

I have written out the poem in my best handwriting (which is pretty good, except for "f"s which I always make too lumpy) and done a border in rainbow colours with pictures of cupcakes and sort of bow things. Altogether I think I have done a very good job.

Of course it's not true. Not even one bit. Well, apart from the homework, sometimes.

It was Bella's idea. Bella is my best friend. She is still my best friend even though she has moved

2

about a thousand miles away to live on a goat farm in Wales. Bella is very good at ideas and making you feel better, which is one of the reasons I miss her a lot. Luckily we get to chat online most nights, especially as I am always needing advice on how to deal with my weird family.

Like earlier this evening.

Mum was in the kitchen doing experiments with food – she calls this cooking but no one else does. She has decided that we need to eat more healthily and also that we need to spend less money (to be honest, she decides this about every twenty minutes). She got a free magazine from the supermarket called *Fabulous Frugal Food* which apparently tells you how to cook mouth-watering family meals for next to nothing. I am thinking of writing to the supermarket and telling them to take out the word "Fabulous" because they could be done for false advertising.

The trouble is my mum hasn't really got past the "pasta bake" recipe on page one. We have had pasta bake three times this week already.

"They are different types of pasta bake, Emily," Mum said, but apart from two being dried up and one being gloopy I haven't really noticed any difference. And whatever sort of pasta bake it is, it's mostly made out of courgettes anyway because my mum has grown about a gazillion of them in the back garden. Apparently just because she has grown them, we now have to eat them. All of them.

I was just trying to look through the oven door to see if tonight's pasta bake was the dry or gloopy variety, when Mum casually announced, "I'm going to start an allotment club at school, Emily."

"A what?" I said, straightening up too quickly and banging my head on the oven door handle.

"An allotment club. I've spoken to Mr Meakin about it, he thinks it's an excellent idea.  We'll dig up a patch of the school field and plant things. It will be fun."

"Who will? What do you mean?" My head was hurting but I wasn't sure if that was from bumping my head on the door handle or trying to understand what Mum was saying.

"Us! I've been thinking about it for a while." She pulled a gloopy-variety pasta bake from the oven and frowned at it as if it had done something it shouldn't.

"But why?" I asked.

"Children need to learn where their food comes from."

And I thought, *That's easy if you live in our house – it mostly comes from page one of* Fabulous Frugal Food.

"When you say 'us', Mum, who do you mean

exactly?" I said, getting a horrible feeling at the bottom of my tummy.

"Us! All the children in Allotment Club ... and you, of course. I will need you to be my assistant," she said, shoving a handful of cutlery at me and waving towards the table.

"No way, Mum! I don't do mud. Or clubs. And definitely not clubs with mud."

Mum fixed me with a firm stare. "Emily, I am relying on you to help out."

"But I can't, Mum. It will be ... it will be ... humiliating!"

"Don't be silly. It will be good for me to get out of the house, put on my wellies and do a bit of exercise. And Clover will enjoy the fresh air and it will be good for the environment and the school – it's a win, win, win, win!"

"Win, win, win, win, lose! You forgot the lose bit – my bit!"

"I would have thought you'd be pleased you have a mum who takes an interest in the environment," she said, noisily clattering the dinner plates on to the table.

I am not sure why anyone would be pleased to have a mum who takes an interest in the environment. My mum has been taking an interest in the environment for weeks now and all it seems to mean is that I have to walk to school in the rain because she has sold her car. Not that it matters, as half the time my school uniform is already damp because Mum thinks our tumble dryer is personally responsible for melting the polar ice caps.

"But you can't come to my school in your scarecrow outfit and dig up the school field. It's probably illegal. You could get arrested for damaging school property." I looked around for reinforcements but there was only my baby sister, Clover, in her bouncy chair, and Dad, who had just wandered in and was looking suspiciously at the cooker.

I decided Dad was the slightly better option. "Dad. Say something. Tell Mum she can't humiliate me in front of the whole school."

Dad took a breath to say something but Mum thumped a huge pasta bake in the middle of the table and Dad closed his mouth again and just looked worried.

"And it is not a scarecrow outfit, Emily," Mum said after a slight pause to see if anyone was going to be brave enough to complain about the pasta bake. "I will be wearing my gardening clothes because I will be creating a new school vegetable patch, which is a very positive move to teach healthy eating. Jamie Oliver would be proud," she said, and dolloped a lump of pasta bake on to my plate. And I thought, *It's a pity that my mum can't pay more attention to Jamie Oliver when she is doing the actual cooking.*

So now you see why I had to speak to Bella.

Tonight's chat:

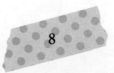

Emily says: BELLA!!!!!!!!

 Bella says: Hi. What's up?

 Emily says: I am sooooo glad
u r there - my mum has gone
bonkers.

 Bella says: That happened a
long time ago, Emily.

 Emily says: But she's going
to go to school and dig up the
field and grow vegetables!

 Bella says: Nooooo!

 Emily says: And she's going to
wear her scarecrow outfit!

 Bella says: Not your dad's old
jumper and that hat!

 Emily says: Yessssssss!

Bella says: Nooooooo!

 Emily says: And wellies.

 Bella says: Not the pink
wellies with the poodles on?

 Emily says: Yesssssss!

 Bella says: Nooooooo!

 Emily says: And she's going to
make me help her and my wellies
are from when I was in Year
Four and have got ladybirds
on.

 Bella says: Nooooooo!

(I was hoping she was going to get on to the
good advice bit soon because so far she hadn't been
very helpful.)

10

Emily says: Why can't I have normal parents?

 Bella says: There's no such thing. All parents are weird.

(Which is true in her case. I mean, what sort of mum and dad move their family to Wales to raise goats? Now that's really poor parenting.)

 Emily says: I just want a mum who bakes cakes and wears nice clothes.

 Bella says: I just want a mum who doesn't smell of goats.

Emily says: One who can't be bothered with the environment.

 Bella says: You should write a list. My Perfect Mother.

Emily says: LOL. But really, what shall I do?

 Bella says: Well . . . you could start by buying her some new wellies.

Bella wasn't as helpful as usual tonight. Maybe she is spending too much time with the goats.

Mum and Dad were upstairs trying to get Clover bathed. It takes two of them and even then they don't manage very well. Most of the water seems to end up on them. I thought I'd better start my literacy homework quickly in case they called me to help hold the soap or something. Mrs

Lovetofts, our teacher, has given up on Tudors for a bit. She says she's too exhausted after the Tudor Times Time-Travel Trip we went on recently. She has given us some different writing to do:

"Write about something you couldn't manage without."

I thought I would write about my Wavey Cat, which Bella gave me before she left. It's a white china cat with a wavey paw. It is supposed to bring you good luck and grant wishes but it is a bit hit and miss. Still, I love it. It's a bit like having Bella around even when she's not. I got a piece of paper and wrote "My Wavey Cat" at the top. Then I felt like it was probably time to take a study break.

I flicked Wavey Cat's paw

and said, "Please can I have a perfect mother." And then the thought popped into my head – *write a list* – just like Bella was saying it. Weird.

So I thought, *Why not? What if I wrote a list and left it lying around for my mum to find? Maybe something would sink in. What a brilliant idea!* Bella did give me good advice. I just wasn't paying attention. And I took another piece of paper and wrote:

My Perfect Mother:
cake baker
biscuit maker
great cook
cares about how she looks . . .

which was funny because it started to rhyme – and then I had a flash of Emily Sparkes creativityness and

 turned it into a poem. Which was really fun and I can't wait to show Bella because she will think it's a good laugh, and I am going to leave it on the kitchen table so my mum can see it and gain some valuable insights into how a proper parent should behave. And now I have to totally finish my literacy homework.

CHAPTER TWO

Domestic ~~Bliss~~ Miss

Monday Morning

 I am eating my Coco-Crispies in front of breakfast TV. This is clearly not a good start to the school day and if any education experts are reading this they will most probably be horrified, but that's how things are in our house these days. My dad has already gone to work and my mum is upstairs looking after my baby sister. When it comes to providing the most important meal of the day, I am expected to totally fend for myself – again.

I don't mind too much, though, because Dana Devene is on breakfast TV this morning. She is their homes and lifestyles guru (though I have no idea what a *guru* is). She also does this programme called *Dana Devene, Domestic Queen*, which I sometimes watch after school. I think Dana Devene is very talented. She is brilliant at making things like cushion covers and curtains and her house is all beautiful and proper – not like ours, which is a general disaster area. This morning Dana is showing everyone how to bake cherry iced cookies. She has chosen cherries and icing because they will match the red and white tablecloth she is using today. See what I mean? Simple but effective.

I don't think we have a tablecloth.

"These just need to go in the oven for a few

minutes," says Dana. "Time to remind you that tomorrow is the last day for entries to our competition, Mum in a Million. Tell us why your mum deserves the star prize – a total makeover!"

There is a lot of "Oooing" and "Aaahing" from the other presenters and then Dana goes off to get her cookies from the oven.

I don't get to see the final cookies, though, because I am utterly distracted by the letterbox which has just gone *flap*. There is a postcard on the floor with a picture of a hammock swinging between palm trees under a blue sky. It is addressed to:

Miss E. Sparkes
(the one who
is 11 and can't
bake cakes, in
case the baby has got an "E" name
too – AT LAST).

It is from Chloe Clarke, who is a very annoying person and always seems to end up being my friend even when I don't want her to be.

It's all go in Goa!
Sun, sand, sea, swimming, surfing and so not school!
Mum and Chuck love it so much they are thinking about buying the hotel, so I won't be back anytime soon.
Hope you're having fun with rain, homework and Tudors and stuff.
Totes see you laters!
Chloe xoxoxo
PS. Olly & Jessie send their love

I suppose Chloe is lying back in the sun, sipping pineapple juice through a straw, while I am sitting here watching the rain run down the window and eating Coco-Crispies (which have now turned into Coco-Soggies) and worrying about my mum utterly embarrassing me to pieces in front of the whole school. It doesn't really matter if Chloe stays in India or not because she is not coming back to our school anyway. She is going to go to Magnolia Hall, which is a school for rich people where normal people are not allowed. Really, it is not fair because I am a totally nice person but Chloe is getting all the fun – and things are not supposed to work that way. The main trouble with Chloe is that you are never sure if she's telling the truth, and she is very good at getting other people into trouble in an accidentally-on-purpose kind of way. So I am sort of glad she's not coming back, but also sort of not, because I've definitely got a bit of a shortage in the friends department.

I am just in the middle of a big sigh about how unfair life is (already, and I have only had eleven years of it – imagine how much worse it could get) when there is a very loud, old-fashioned sort of beeping sound, which means I have got a text. It is loud and old-fashioned because my mobile is loud and old-fashioned. It's massive and bright yellow. It used to belong to my dad and was probably the first attempt at a replacement for the carrier pigeon.

Did U read Chloe's postcard yet???

My new, *second*-best friend, Zuzanna. How does she know I got a postcard? She must be spying on our letterbox.

I text back:

> Yeah. She is really in Goa.
> How do you knoa?

Which I think is funny and because poetry is totally my new thing.

Even though I am texting this I still find it all a bit difficult to believe. Chloe really is in India. I mean, I know she said she was going but you can never be sure with Chloe. It's only been two weeks since she was sitting in a Tudor field dressed as a raspberry pavlova.

My phone beeps again:

Knoa? You mean know?

Zuzanna has a bit of a thing about spelling. I wonder if it is worth explaining to her that it was meant to be a joke, but I don't bother because even though she's very nice, she's not very imaginative or creative and she gets a bit stressed when I am.

My phone beeps again. Zuzanna is definitely a bit het up this morning:

And who are Jessie and Olly????

I am just looking around the room to see if there is some sort of hidden camera through which Zuzanna is managing to read my postcard, when I realise that she must have had a postcard too. Which makes me feel a tiny bit annoyed, because even though Zuzanna and I are now friends and have both decided we don't like Chloe *at all* – I still want Chloe to like me the best.

"Emily!" my mum yells from upstairs. "I hope you're not on your phone."

I swear she can see through floors.

"No," I yell back while speed texting:

Got to go.

Sending messages in the morning is banned in our house. Sending messages after school is fine, but there is a total morning exclusion zone. It doesn't make sense to me but in our house once Mum's declared it as "a rule", you're stuck with it.

Our house is a dictatorship really, like North Korea but with less marching.

I quickly stick the phone in the fruit bowl where it sits alongside two shrivelled apples and does a very good impression of a banana. Just in time, as Mum comes in carrying Clover. "Emily, what *are* you doing?" she says. (Mum, I mean, not Clover. She can only say "waaaah" and very occasionally "goo".) "You're not even dressed yet!" I don't point out that my mum is actually still in pyjamas herself because that would start another lecture about how much she has to cope with.

"I can't find my school skirt," I say. "It's not anywhere." Then immediately wish I hadn't, because Mum says, "It must be *somewhere*, Emily." Sometimes I think parents must go to special classes to learn how to say really annoying, predictable things.

The trouble is there's a bit of a washing issue going on in our house at the moment, and the issue is that the washing is not going on, if you see what I mean. Really, Mum is at home all day with just a tiny baby to look after so you would think she'd get right on top of the housework, but, since Clover was born, she does seem to have let her standards slip (and Gran says they weren't that high in the first place).

"Have you looked in your wardrobe?" Mum asks, which is a bit pointless because we both know there is nothing actually hanging up in my wardrobe except an age-14 shirt Mum bought me by accident when I was nine. (Hang in there, shirt, only another three years to go.) Everything else is either on the floor of the wardrobe because it fell off the hanger, or in a pile on the dressing table waiting to be put on a hanger so it can also have a turn at falling off. It's not my fault. The rail has been wonky for ages but nothing in our house ever gets fixed.

"Yes, it's not there."

"Well . . . well . . . go and have another look."

Which means I now *have* to go and double check, because if Mum goes up and finds it she will just stand there holding it out with her lips pursed, saying nothing in a really annoying way. So I do my best stompy walk upstairs, just to show I am under protest.

 I have a quick look in my wardrobe and it's definitely not there so I am just having a big rummage through the pile of clothes on the dressing table when Mum comes in behind me. "Emily!" she snaps. "I folded all those clothes – now look at them!"

Which is a very unreasonable attitude coming from a mother whose child has had to search the house from top to bottom for at least several minutes just to find something to clothe herself in.

"Go and look on the airer," she sighs.

"Goo," says Clover, which is not fair because now they are ganging up on me.

The clothes airer is in the living room, right in front of the window (and I really hope no one from school walks past because there are two pairs of my dad's big pants right near the front). My mum's tumble dryer phobia means that most days our living room looks like a damp jumble sale. But my school skirt is not on the airer, and now there are only about six minutes left and even I am starting to think I might be late. You might not think that being a couple of minutes late matters, but that is because you don't have Zuzanna as your second-best friend. Zuzanna is always on time. She waits outside her house for me to arrive and I can tell exactly how many minutes late I am by how much she is frowning when I get there.

"Mum, I really can't find anything to wear!" I call

up the stairs and I am nearly blinded by a flying school dress smacking me in the face.

"You'll have to wear your summer dress," yells Mum, not in the least bit concerned that she could have just caused a serious medical incident.

"But it's October!"

"Well, wear this," she shouts and makes another attempt on my life with a low-flying school cardie.

There is no more time to argue though. If I don't leave by exactly 8.27 a.m., Zuzanna will be frowning like a gorilla who's had her banana nicked.

I pull on the dress and cardie, grab my bag and coat and head for the door.

"Homework!" yells Mum, seeing through the floor again.

I swerve back round past the dining table and grab my homework.

"Bye," calls my mum as I open the door. "Have a nice day." Like she hasn't noticed that it's already too late for that.

It is like this all the time in my house now. Since my baby sister was born my mum and dad have been mostly useless at being parents. They are always tired and busy.

Like last night I only wanted my mum to get me a biscuit and a drink while I was watching TV and she said, "Emily, you can get it yourself. You are eleven, you know."

"Yes," I said, "I am eleven, not *eleventeen*!" which didn't make sense so I ended up losing the argument on a technicality.

Mum has even stopped bothering to walk me to school. She says I'm old enough to walk with Zuzanna now, which is good, but a bit stressful.

Zuzanna is standing outside the shiny blue door of her neat and tidy house, with an expression that is about 3.5 on the frowning scale. Not too bad.

"Why are you wearing a summer dress?" she says as I run up to her.

"Mum had a bit of a washing disaster."

"But it's October," Zuzanna says, her frown going up to a 4.8.

"Did you get a postcard too?" I say, waving my card at her and trying to change the subject.

We walk to school and Zuzanna shows me her postcard, which has the same words as mine but a slightly different picture. Her hammock has a pillow on it.

"It looks like a lovely place, doesn't it?" Zuzanna says. "So relaxing . . . especially on my card."

"Yes, though I don't think you need a pillow on a hammock. I mean, mine looks really comfortable as it is."

"Oh yes, but it would be lovely, wouldn't it, lying on a hammock in the sun . . . with a pillow."

"Why don't you go to Goa then?" I say in a more snappy way than I meant, but I do secretly wish I had a pillow too.

"Don't be silly, Emily," Zuzanna says as she pushes open the school door. "I'd miss *X Factor*."

CHAPTER THREE

Surprise, Surprise!

Monday – School

Mrs Lovetofts, our very cheerful teacher, is already in class, making a display of our Tudor-style cross-stitch bookmarks. Zuzanna's is at the top in the middle because she has done a Tudor Rose, which is very neat and Tudorish and looks exactly like a rose, and has the words *Tudor Rose* stitched across the top just in case you still don't get it.

My bookmark was meant to be a poppy but by the time I got to the thread box there was no red thread left, so I had to do it glittery purple. And then when I went to get green for the stem, there was only orange left, so it looks a bit like a Tudor firework. Mrs Lovetofts has put it near the side at the bottom.

When she has finished stapling, Mrs Lovetofts claps her hand together. "Everyone should be sitting down by now. Nicole, could you collect up the homework, please?"

"But she did it last time, Miss," Babette says as Nicole walks past giving her a smug smile. It's amazing the amount of things the twins find to argue about.

Zuzanna and I are already sitting down. Zuzanna is very organised and has her book and pencil case out on the table when most people are still trying to remember where they sit. I am trying to be more like Zuzanna but I have not got off to a good start as I have left my pencil case on the kitchen table.

"Can I borrow a pen?" I ask.

Zuzanna gives me a slightly disappointed look and says, "Really, Emily. You need to get more organised." She gives me her Colchester Zoo pen.

 "You can keep it," she says. "I don't like it because part of the picture has rubbed off and it looks like the zebra's got no legs."

"You could just pretend it's a seahorse," I say, but I get another frown which makes me think maybe I am being too creative again.

"Right, everyone. I have some very exciting news," Mrs Lovetofts says. "Gavin has not sat down yet."

I know Mrs Lovetofts gets excited about everything from a new library book to a change in the school lunch menu, but this sounds like a first even for her. Then I realise this is not the news, but is her nice way of telling Gross-Out Gavin to stop showing Alfie Balfour his impression of an undead-corpse-type person and to go back to his chair. We all have to wait for him to do a zombie-style walk over to his table and sit down with his head on one side and his tongue hanging out.

"As I was saying, some exciting news." Mrs Lovetofts smiles her great big smile, like she's about to announce an extra bank holiday. "This week we are going to start a new mini-topic!"

"But we haven't finished Tudors yet," Gross-Out Gavin says. "I want to do the bit where they all get plague and bits start falling off them." He leaps up and does an impression of a Tudor with bits falling off, which is very similar to a zombie. In fact, I think he might still be doing a zombie and trying to fool us, but Mrs Lovetofts tells him to sit down again so I haven't got much time to decide.

"Mr Meakin has decided that the school has covered the Tudor era in quite sufficient detail for now. Our new topic is going to be" – she claps her hands together excitedly – "Harvest!"

There is a bit of groaning but Mrs Lovetofts smiles through it as usual. I don't really see how Harvest can be a topic, it's just food. It's like my mum saying, "Kids need to learn where their food comes from." Why? As long as you can tell the difference between stuff you can eat and stuff you can't, then what more do you need to know? Although as I am thinking this I notice that Alfie Balfour is chewing a purple crayon and I think maybe Mrs Lovetofts has a point after all (which is more than the crayon does now).

"We will be talking about food, how it grows, and looking at traditional harvesting methods, and of course we will be having our own Juniper

 Road Primary Harvest Festival! Any questions?"

"Yes, Miss," Gross-Out Gavin says. "Could we do Harvest with just a little bit of plague?"

At lunch Zuzanna and I are sitting on the ENDSHIP SEA, my favourite bench in the playground. It used to be called the FRIENDSHIP SEAT but some of the letters fell off. Me and Bella always liked ENDSHIP SEA better anyway. It sounds kind of exciting. Zuzanna is not excited, however. She is moaning about the weather, which is a bit grey and cold.

"What do you think Chloe is doing now?" Zuzanna says. "Sitting on a beach?"

I look at my limp tuna sandwich. "Probably, and drinking coconut juice and eating mango slices."

"With the waves gently lapping her toes," Zuzanna says as it starts to rain.

We both sigh. Chloe Clarke told us so many tall stories and confusing lies that it doesn't seem fair that we end up sitting in the drizzle while she has fun in the sun. On the other hand, I can't help missing her. She definitely made life more interesting.

"I wonder if we'll ever see her again," I say.

 "I shouldn't think so," Zuzanna says. "She might end up staying in India to run a hotel."

"Or come back to Magnolia Hall, her exclusive private school."

"With cookery lessons by Jamie Oliver." Zuzanna laughs and we both start giggling.

"And archery with Jessica Ennis," I say, and then we are doubled up with laughter. "No," I manage to splutter, "I think we've definitely seen the last of Chloe Clarke."

Which is like one of those things they say in films just before a big surprise, so I should really be able to predict what happens next.

"Yoohoo! Girls. Suurpriiise!!" shrieks a familiar voice from the other side of the playground. Zuzanna and I look up and I drop my tuna sandwich in shock. It can't be . . . she left, she's not coming back, she's supposed to be in Goa!

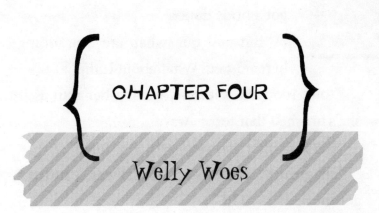

CHAPTER FOUR

Welly Woes

Monday - Still School

Zuzanna has taken off her glasses and is polishing them furiously, but there is no mistaking Chloe Clarke waving and hurrying over to meet us.

"Hi, girls!" she says breathlessly, hugging us both at once.

"Chloe?" Zuzanna says, which is at least more than I can manage.

"Corrrrect!" Chloe says. "Unless I've got a body double."

"But ... but what are you doing here?" I say. "What about India?"

"Totes too hot," she says, waving her arm as if she's brushed that topic away.

"But I thought you were getting a hotel?"

"Oh great, you got my postcard. I wasn't sure if I got the address right."

"But – how? What?" I have so many questions that I can't seem to think straight, so I just say, "Are you back for good?"

"Just for now," she says, "until I start—"

"Mag Hall?" Zuzanna and I say together, and Chloe nods happily.

"Now let me tell you all about Goa," she says. "You won't belieeeeeve what happened."

Chloe is halfway through a long story about sitting on the aeroplane next to Olly Murs and Jessie J and how they ended up staying in the same

42

hotel and singing at her mum's honeymoon party when Zuzanna suddenly says, "Who is that strange person on the school field?"

Chloe looks to where she is pointing and says, "More importantly, what are they wearing? Totes fashion disaster!"

"It looks a bit suspicious to me," Zuzanna says. "Is that a tape measure they're using? I wonder if they have permission to measure school property. Perhaps we'd better tell someone." She looks around for a teacher to tell and I quickly grab her arm.

"Oh, it's probably just some weird new teaching assistant," I say, "with extra measuring duties. Come on, let's go in, it's starting to rain."

 "It's been raining for twenty minutes, Emily," Zuzanna says, who has probably been timing it, but she picks up her lunchbox and follows me in.

"Wait up, girls," Chloe says, running along behind. "I haven't got to the good part yet!"

But I am rushing for the door and definitely not looking back towards the school field where a woman in pink poodle wellies is leaning on her spade.

On the way to class we pass the school noticeboard in the corridor and I stop and stare at a new poster:

Allotment Club
Thursday lunchtimes on the field
Come and have some fun digging and planting
Everyone welcome.
Sign below:

Luckily I seem to be in time and no one has signed it yet. Sorry, Mum, but this calls for some instant Emily Sparkes action – now!

I can't pull the poster down straight away because Zuzanna and Chloe will notice. The

44

only thing I can think of to do is to stand in front of it.

"Are you coming?" Zuzanna says as I stand with my back against the noticeboard.

"Err, not right now," I say. "I, erm ... was just looking at that picture."

I point at a faded watercolour of some fishing boats on the opposite wall that has been there since I first started school and probably for about four hundred years before that. "I've never really noticed it before."

Zuzanna looks at the picture and then looks at me like I've gone a bit mad, then Chloe comes up and links arms with her and says, "I soooo have to tell you about the hotel disco. It was totes amaze!" and they go into class together.

It seems like an hour till the buzzer finally goes and it has been very difficult standing in the same spot, especially as it is right in front of the noticeboard and it seems that everyone wants to look at something today, when normally no one ever does. Joshua wants to sign up for football practice, which is not too bad because I just have to move my elbow up so he can write his name on the list, but when Small Emily B wants to see what the vegetarian option is for tomorrow's lunch I virtually have to do an impression of an exceptionally bendy flamingo standing on one leg with its neck under its wing and even then she has to go on tiptoes. It is all very exhausting and I am utterly weak by the time the buzzer finally goes. I wait for the corridor to empty and I put my hands up behind my back, pull the poster down and stuff it up my school cardigan before strolling innocently into class.

Amy-Lee Langer comes in just behind me and makes a grab for her lunchbox. "I'm starving," she says. "I can't believe I got a lunchtime detention just for telling those Reception kids that there's a zombie teacher who lives in the caretaker's cupboard. Like, they must be stupid if they believe that."

"Yeah," Yeah-Yeah Yasmin says.

"They *are* only four," Zuzanna says.

"I was teaching them creative storytelling," Amy-Lee says.

Everyone seems very excited that Chloe has come back. Joshua is doing his usual gazing at her like she's an angel from heaven – I am not sure how anyone could make that mistake. Daniel Waller is managing to smile and look like he's about to cry at the same time. Gracie McKenzie and Small Emily B are asking her about her holiday and getting all the details about Olly and Jessie. The twins, Babette and Nicole, are the only ones not looking pleased to see Chloe. They don't like it that Chloe can speak French better than they can (which is not saying much, really).

"But I thought you were going back to your old school, Rag Hall," Babette says. Nicole nods in agreement, which is actually quite amazing because they never agree on anything.

"*Mag* Hall," Chloe says. "I'm considering it."

"Well, I wouldn't want to go there," Amy-Lee Langer says through a mouthful of bread roll. "Sounds like it's full of posh kids."

"Yeah," says Yeah-Yeah Yasmin.

"I don't think that's something you have to worry about too much," Chloe says, smiling at her sweetly.

"Yeah," says Alfie, "you have to be rich to go there, don't you?"

"Of course," Chloe says.

"How do you know I'm not rich?" Amy-Lee says, glaring at him.

"Yeah," says Yeah-Yeah Yasmin.

"If you're rich, I must be a king or something," Gross-Out says.

"Well, try this for a crown," Amy-Lee says and squashes her left-over fish paste roll on his head. Unfortunately for her, Mrs Lovetofts has just come in. "Amy-Lee!" she says. "If you don't want your lunch, please put it in the bin, not on someone's head. Lunchtime detention tomorrow."

Sometimes I wonder if Amy-Lee knows what a normal lunchtime is like.

Mrs Lovetofts tells everyone to sit down, then remembers she has left her bag in the staff room and goes off to get it again.

I make a bit of crunchy noise as I sit down. Zuzanna gives me a funny look but fortunately Chloe says, "I still haven't told you what happened to Olly Murs' flip-flops," and Zuzanna is distracted again.

I don't join in the conversation because I am

49

worn out by all my efforts and have to have a totally big rest for a few minutes. I wish I had a normal mother.

Because Mrs Lovetofts is too nice to be a teacher,  she has made a very poor decision and allowed Chloe to come and sit on the end of our table and be a three with me and Zuzanna. This means that Chloe will now have two people to talk to all the time when she is supposed to be listening.

"So what happened to your mum and step-dad getting a hotel?" Zuzanna is saying. "You said you were going to stay in India."

"I didn't say I was definitely going to – I said they were thinking about it, which they were, but now they're not," Chloe says.

"So are you staying at this school?" I say.

"Hmm . . . it's an either, or situation."

"Either, or?"

"Yes, either I stay or I don't."

"But don't you—" but I don't get to finish my sentence because Chloe suddenly lets out one of her louder shrieks.

"OMG! That scarecrow person is now totes digging up the school field!"

Everyone rushes to the window to look. My mum is standing in the corner of the field in pink wellies, my dad's old jumper and a flat cap my granddad used to wear before it got too old-fashioned for him.

Clover is in her buggy with the rain splashing off the cover while my mum digs up clumps of mud and grass.

"That's got to be against school rules," Zuzanna says.

"It must be for the new Allotment Club," Nicole says.

"Allotment Club. Err ... what's that?" I say, crackling suspiciously.

"There's a poster on the Key Stage One noticeboard," says Babette.

Another poster! I should have thought of that. My heart sinks. I have another poster to get down before I've even managed to get this one out from up the back of my cardie.

"All the Year Twos are signing up," Nicole says.

"Not *all* of them," Babette says.

"Who is that digging anyway?" Chloe says. "He looks sort of familiar."

"He?" Zuzanna says. "It must be a woman. Look at the pink wellies."

"It's got to be a man," Chloe says. "I mean, what sort of woman would wear that hat?"

"So, Chloe," I say, grabbing her by the elbow and guiding her away from the window, "tell me some more about your mum's honeymoon."

Chloe beams at me and starts off on another long story about how Jessie J heard her singing karaoke and will probably get her a recording deal.

I am pretending to listen and trying to get her

back to the desk and to stop the poster falling out of my cardigan and beginning to feel very stressed when luckily Mrs Lovetofts gets back and makes everyone come away from the window and sit down.

"Miss," I say, "do you mind if I pull the blind down on that window? The sun's getting in my eyes."

"Sun?" Mrs Lovetofts says. "It's raining, Emily. Well, actually it might be a good idea as I have something to put up on the white board."

I rush to the window and get one last glimpse of my mum chucking a spadeful of soil into a wheelbarrow before I pull down the blind sharply. I really need to do some total Emily Sparkes creative thinking.

CHAPTER FIVE

I'm a Poet and Everyone Knows It

Monday - Still School

"Now, class," Mrs Lovetofts says, "I have something I want to show you. I have just been having a look through some of your homework: *The Thing I Couldn't Manage Without.*

"There was some very nice, imaginative work. Nicole, it was lovely to hear that you couldn't manage without your sister, although I'm not sure that your number one reason should have been 'because she makes me look better when I stand next to her'. And, Alfie, I was intrigued to know that you couldn't manage without a few elastic bands in case of an emergency. But you didn't really explain what sort of emergency you might use them for. Perhaps if you needed to hold together something that was broken?"

"Maybe, Miss," says Alfie, "but mostly just to ping at people," and he demonstrates on the side of Gross-Out's head.

"Yes, well, as I said, very imaginative, but there was one that stood out above the others this time and I'd like to share it with you."

Mrs Lovetofts fiddles with the laptop and the whiteboard and then gets Joshua to come and help her and finally up flashes a familiar poem:

My Perfect Mother

My mum is so fantastic, she makes
cakes and cleans and cooks,
   She does the washing and the ironing
and cares about her looks.
   She wears such lovely dresses
and arranges pretty flowers,
   She helps me with my
homework or sits and sews for
hours.
   Her hair is soft and shiny, it's
pretty and it's curled,
   She bakes me cookies after school, yes, she's
definitely the best mum in the world.

"OM *actual* G! Who wrote that?"
Chloe says. "It's totally ...
totally ... cringe-omatic!"
   "Yuck. It's making

me feel ill," Amy-Lee says. Then she looks over at Chloe and adds, "Totally."

"Yeah," Yeah-Yeah Yasmin says.

"And the last line doesn't scan properly," Zuzanna says.

I don't have time to say anything as I am hurriedly sliding under the table.

Mrs Lovetofts claps her hands together and beams her big smile. "What a wonderful poem," she says, pointing to where it is displayed in massive letters to the whole class. "Well done, Emily Sparkes. You clearly couldn't do without your mother, although I'm not sure that she counts as a 'thing' but never mi— err . . . where is Emily?"

"She's under the table, Miss," Zuzanna says, which is *exactly* why she is my *second*-best friend. Bella always knew what to do if a teacher asked an awkward question – shrug your shoulders and suddenly look interested in your pencil case. Unfortunately Bella is currently only knowing what to do in Wales.

I examine the floor for any cracks that might helpfully open up and swallow me whole but there aren't any so I sit there for a few seconds while Mrs Lovetofts says, "Emily? Are you OK, Emily?" Until I have no choice but to slowly climb back up on to my chair with Mum's poster making crunchy noises up my cardie.

"Ah, there you are, Emily. What a super poem you've written. Clearly you 'couldn't manage without' your mum – very well done!"

How could this happen? I did my homework on Wavey Cat . . . I must have picked up the poem instead of my homework this morning!

I can feel everyone in the room looking at me and I am trying to avoid catching anyone's eye, although I can't help noticing Gross-Out as he sticks his fingers in his throat and pretends that reading my poem is making him feel sick.

"That poem is totes terrible," whispers Chloe, "and nothing like your mum. I mean, she's nice enough, but like no way does she care about her looks."

"She does sometimes," I say, trying to banish the pink wellies from my mind.

Zuzanna leans over and whispers, "And I'm sorry, Emily, I mean, your mum is very kind but she so can't cook – when I came round she burnt the ice-cream!"

"She didn't burn it, she melted it."

"She set fire to the tub."

"It was an accident!" I say, too loudly, and Mrs Lovetofts raises her eyebrows in my general direction, which is probably the worst telling-off she has ever given me.

"Look," I mutter, "I know the poem's not true. It was only meant to be a joke."

"Well, basically you have lied in your homework," Chloe says. "Really, Emily, you should always try to tell the truth."

And at that point I can't think of anything else to say, so I just ignore them and sit there trying not to crackle.

After school Mrs Lovetofts asks me to stay behind a second, which is very annoying as I was hoping to sneak the poster into the bin while everyone was rushing out.

"I love this poem, Emily," she says. "It's lovely that someone appreciates their mother; lots of children don't."

I give her a half smile. "She's definitely a very unusual sort of mum."

"Exactly, which is why I want you to know that

I've entered it into a competition. Do you know *Dana Devene, Domestic Queen*?"

"Err . . . yes."

"Isn't she marvellous?" Mrs Lovetofts goes a bit dreamy for a moment and then says, "Well, she's doing a competition to find a Mum in a Million. It sounds as if your mum is a very good candidate."

"Well, err . . ." Sometimes I think "Well" and "Err" are pretty much all I say to teachers.

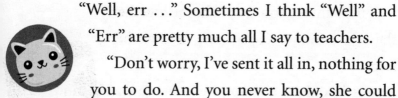

"Don't worry, I've sent it all in, nothing for you to do. And you never know, she could win the top prize! A complete makeover – hair, nails, clothes, everything! I'm sure she'd love that."

Which just goes to show how much teachers know.

"Well, I must get on," Mrs Lovetofts says, gathering up her folders, and she walks out of the classroom muttering, "Whatever is that funny crackling sound?"

I walk over to the bin to

get rid of the very itchy and annoying poster. Just as I pull it out from the back of my cardie I hear a voice from the door saying, "Hello, love!" and I have to quickly stuff it back up again.

"Oh. Hi, Mum," I say, turning round to see her standing there with her baggy jumper, flat cap and now extremely dirty pink poodle wellies.

"I thought we could walk home together," she says, smiling through the mud on her face.

And I think,

a. I am very glad everyone else has gone home already, and,

b. a complete makeover would be an excellent idea.

CHAPTER SIX

Unexpected Guests

Monday - Home

If you were an alien (and you might actually be, I suppose, in which case, "Welcome to Earth") and you transported yourself into our living room, just to have a look at how Earthlings live, you would not be hanging around long before you shot back off to Planet Zorg (I have obviously made that name up – you are probably from a planet with a

weird name which can only be smelled and not spoken or something).

Apart from the clothes airer in the front window (fortunately, my dad's pants no longer seem to be at the front, although unfortunately, they have been replaced with his Homer Simpson socks), there is a great big pile of copper pipes stuck across the middle of the floor. This is because my dad is a nervous plumber. He is convinced someone will steal his pipes if he puts them in the garage.

Mum did point out that the garage has a lock but Dad said, "If they can get up on those church roofs they can get anywhere."

Mum said that it was lead that got stolen off church roofs, not copper, but Dad said, "It's all the same," which is a bit worrying when you think he's supposed to be professionally trained.

Every day Dad says he's going to move them, but then doesn't get around to it. They have been there for over six weeks now, which makes them nearly as old as Clover, and I am wondering if we will have to give them names soon too.

And if the copper pipes and damp clothes weren't bad enough, there are also a gazillion baby toys in a pile in the corner, because everyone who comes round thinks they need to bring Clover a cuddly rabbit or plastic sparkly rattle even though she is only really interested in sucking her hand or waving her legs in the air. It is a total waste of money, especially when I haven't even got a proper school drinks bottle.

Mum doesn't seem to notice the chaos much, though. We get home and she parks Clover in the living room in her buggy, which takes up just about the last bit of free space in the room.

"She's sleeping," Mum says. "Can you keep an eye on her while I grab a quick shower?" and she disappears off up the stairs.

I slip into the kitchen and bury the poster at the

bottom of the bin. Then I worry that Mum will still find it because my mum finds everything – well, apart from my school skirt – so I shove some other rubbish on top. It is a relief to get it out, as it was very scratchy and walking around constantly crackling was very embarrassing. At least I have got rid of it without anyone seeing me.

"Gooo," says Clover from her buggy in the living room, and I get the uncomfortable feeling that she has inherited Mum's ability to see through walls.

Seeing as Clover has woken up, I get her out of her buggy to sit on the sofa for one of our chats. I have found that my baby sister is a very good listener and sometimes even gives some wise advice. Before she got a name I used to call her Yoda and I think some of that has rubbed off. I might become a child psychologist.

"So, what did you think of your first experience of Allotment Club?" I ask.

"Blerrr," says Clover. It shows how bad it was if she had to make up a whole new word.

"Yes, I totally agree. Not only is it embarrassing to have a mum wearing poodle wellies and a flat cap, but she also has to do it in front of the whole school, *and* she wants me to join in."

"Blerrr," says Clover.

"Exactly, it must have been very embarrassing for you too. I bet Gran wouldn't be impressed. Come to think of it, that's not a bad idea . . ."

I put Clover into her bouncy baby chair and get my banana phone out of the fruit bowl.

"We've got some good news," Dad says a little later as we are sitting down for tea. He says it in such a cheery way that it is almost definitely not good news and Mum looks as if she's thinking the same thing.

"Please don't tell me, you're going to start a school plumbing club," I say.

"No, no, nothing like that," Dad says. "It's just that Uncle Clive is coming to stay for a bit."

"What?" I say.

"Not what, who," Dad says. "Uncle Clive."

Mum looks as if "What" was closer to the truth.

Dad avoids looking anyone in the eye by acting very busy dishing out fish and chips. He has put his foot down on the pasta bake tonight, well, not literally or he would have cheese and pasta all over his foot, but he decided we definitely needed a change. Mum usually gets annoyed about take-away food but tonight she seems a bit worn out after her digging day. The news about Uncle Clive seems to be making her more tired.

"He's had a bit of a falling out with Daisy; they are having a trial separation."

Uncle Clive is Dad's younger brother, he is quite nice, but he doesn't say a lot, unless you know about motorbikes.

"It's only for a couple of days," Dad says, "while they work things out."

"Why? Have they had an argument? Are they going to split up?" I ask – which would be a pity because I like Daisy.  She came round once and showed me the tattoo on her leg. It is supposed to be a dragon. I didn't like to say that it looked more like a llama. I'm definitely never getting a tattoo.

"Well, I think it was to do with Uncle Clive's engine oil getting mixed up with Daisy's aromatherapy oils or something. Anyway, I'm sure he won't be staying long."

Mum has been strangely quiet throughout this whole conversation. She's never too keen on having anyone to stay. I am wondering if she has fallen asleep due to all the digging and fresh air, but she is just quietly eating her fish and chips and not looking at me, which is very odd. I am just thinking about this and also thinking, *I suppose it will be OK having Uncle Clive round because he's mostly quite friendly*, when something occurs to me.

"Where is he going to sleep?"

I don't get an answer, though, because the doorbell goes and it is Uncle Clive already.

He is even bigger than I remember, and I am wondering how he and Dad can be brothers when clearly he is related to Hagrid.

"'Ello all," he says. "Sorry to barge in on you like this." He dumps a cardboard box on the kitchen floor and gives my mum a hug which I am worried she may not survive.

"No problem, Clive," Mum says, wrestling her

way out of his grip. "Always room for one more here."

Which there is clearly not.

"And look at the size of Flora," he says.

"Clover," Mum says.

"Oh, yes. Sorry," Uncle Clive says, rubbing Clover's head.

Dad pours Uncle Clive some tea and gives him a packet of biscuits.

Mum clears up all the fish and chip papers and puts them in the bin. Then she hesitates and rummages around a bit and pulls out – the Allotment Club poster!

"How on earth did this get in here?" she says trying to smooth it out. "I don't understand." She sits down again, frowning and looking like she is trying to work something out, and I am very much hoping that she does not work out anything to do with me.

Luckily, Uncle Clive comes to the rescue by

letting out a big sigh that makes everyone jump and Mum spill her tea. "Well, it's very good of you all to let me stay. It should only be for a day or two." He takes a big sip of tea and eats a whole chocolate biscuit in one go. "Although you could persuade me to stay longer," he grins.

Mum does a little choke on her tea and Dad quickly asks about Uncle Clive's motorbike. I help Mum finish clearing up, which is not easy with Uncle Clive taking up most of the space in the kitchen, and twice I nearly trip over his feet, which are far bigger than they need to be.

Dad and Uncle Clive are still talking about motorbikes when I decide it's time to go to see if Bella's online. As I am leaving the kitchen, Uncle Clive looks up. "Oh, Emily. I just wanted to say thanks."

"Thanks?"

"Yes, thanks for letting me borrow your room,

I promise to keep it tidy." He barks with laughter and then he turns back to Dad and says, "So it was the manifold after all . . ."

My room!

Mum gives me a bit of a sheepish look. So that's why she was keeping quiet.

I give Mum a special stare which means *Follow me, now!* and I march into the living room.

Unfortunately Uncle Clive has dumped an enormous rucksack into the last remaining bit of floor space and I stub my toe on it. So instead of giving Mum a cross look I end up doing a sort of embarrassing bunny hop around in circles. And instead of saying, "He can't have my room, that's totally not happening," I say, "Owww! My foot."

Mum seizes her chance to explain. "We thought you could sleep in with Clover for a bit, on a camp bed," she says, dragging the rucksack to one side. "It's only for a couple of nights. It'll be fun."

"Fun?" My mum is so confused about what counts as enjoyable. "Why can't he have Clover's room?" I say.

"Well, he wouldn't fit in the cot," Mum says.

"Not in the cot, on the camp bed I mean."

"Last time he got on the camp bed it collapsed," Mum says with a sigh.

"Hummmmph," I say, which is what you say when you've run out of ideas.

Mum sighs. "Sorry, Emily, you're just going to have to put up with it for a couple of days. If anyone wants me I'll be down in the shed," she calls, heading for the door.

I decide to sulk in my room. Perhaps if I stay in it and refuse to come out then Uncle Clive will have to look elsewhere. It is not that easy trying to find somewhere to sulk, though. My bedroom is not the tidiest place in the world (although it might be one of the tidiest places in our house). I manage to find a space between the broken bookshelf and the box of dusty cuddly toys.

My room hasn't really changed since I was little. It is supposed to be pink, which is bad enough, but that has sort of faded to grey in places. When I was younger my mum painted a big teddy bear on one wall. He is a bit wonky and one of his ears is bigger than the other. I did used to like it but it is embarrassing now. I tried to cover him up with a Taylor Swift poster but you can still see his ears sticking out at the top, which makes Taylor look like she's wearing a Children in Need headband. Also my mum won't let me have a TV in my room because she thinks it will zap my brain cells or something. Really, it is a total disaster bedroom for an eleven-year-old, but the point is it's *my* disaster bedroom, not Uncle Clive's.

I am just thinking that I could slide the dressing

table in front of the door, like they do in films when they are trying to keep the baddies out, when there is a big load of noise downstairs. It's Gran. I decide to give up sulking, which is, anyway, very boring when no one has noticed, and go to find out what all the *palaver* (Gran-speak) is about.

I pass Dad at the bottom of the stairs as he is taking Clover up to bed. "Sorry, Emily," he says. "It's not for long." I give him a look which I hope shows how upset and betrayed I feel, while at the same time showing that I am not the sort of person who lets such things get me down. I'm not sure it works because it looks like he's trying not to laugh.

Gran is already in the kitchen drinking tea and polishing off the rest of the biscuits. She is having a big chat with Uncle Clive about motorbikes, which she doesn't really know much about but my gran can have a chat about anything.

"Yes," she is saying as I walk in, "I told Mrs Humphries, mobility scooters are all very well but you'd collect your pension much quicker if you got one of those Darley Mavison's— Hello, sweetiepie," she says as she sees me. Gran often calls me sweetiepie, except if she's not happy with me, then she calls me "Missus", as in "Come here, Missus, and put this crisp packet in the bin," but I am sweetiepie at the moment so that's good. Well, only a bit good, because now she'll probably want a big hug.

"Come here and give your gran a big hug!" she says, standing up and scraping the chair back. I kind of step towards her but I forget about Uncle Clive's feet, which seem to manage to be in most places at the same time.

I am OK with the tripping over, and even with landing face first in the cardboard box Uncle Clive has left on the floor. But what I am not OK with is being face to face with A RAT!

To be fair, as rats go, it looks quite pleasant – it is

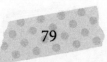

white and sort of cheerful-looking – but it is still a rat and if I look into a box in the kitchen I mostly expect to see Coco-Crispies or biscuits.

I just have time to say, "Eeeeeeeeeeeeeeeeeeeeeeeeek!" before it twitches its pink nose and is off out of the box and across the kitchen floor.

"Lemmy!" calls Uncle Clive and makes a dive to catch it, but it is too quick and disappears behind the fridge.

"Are you all right, sweetiepie?" Gran says, giving me a hand up. "You are an old clumsy pants. Now where's my hug?" She gives me a big fluffy hug that smells like flowers with a bit of broccoli and then says, "Oooh, I've got something for you. Just a minute. I'll get my bag," and she goes out to the hall.

Uncle Clive stops crawling around the floor and looks at me. "She didn't see him, did she?"

"I don't think so," I say.

"Good," he says, and starts peering under the fridge.

"Err ... Uncle Clive?"

"Yep," he says without looking up.

"I hope you don't think this is a rude question, but why have you brought a rat with you?"

Uncle Clive lets out a big sigh and says, "Daisy won't look after him. She said if I go, the rat goes. Sometimes she can be very unreasonable. Thing is, I'm not sure your mum will want him here either. I haven't got round to asking her yet."

"I'm pretty sure she won't want him behind the fridge."

"Oh dear," he says. "Lemmy's such a great pet, except he does like to escape. Look, you won't say anything will you? I'll catch him soon. I don't want your mum to call the ... the pest control people." He shakes his head as if he can't believe anyone would do such a cruel thing.

"Don't worry. I won't say anything. I'll help you catch him if you like."

"Thanks, Emily," Uncle Clive says. "You're a pal," and he slaps me on the back and knocks me into the cooker.

Gran comes back in and says, "I've brought some garibaldis, they're Emily's favourites. Put the kettle on, someone."

Uncle Clive goes to fill the kettle while Gran says, "Now, Emily. What's all this allotment club nonsense you were texting about?"

{ CHAPTER SEVEN }

Poster Problems

Tuesday

The next morning I meet Zuzanna outside her house to walk to school (two minutes late, frown scale 3.1).

"Found your school skirt, then?" she says.

"Yes, it was in the ironing pile."

"Your mum should get an ironing lady. My mum takes everything to a lady at number seven and she does the lot."

"I'm not sure we could afford it, seeing as we also need a cooking, cleaning and washing lady." *And possibly a rat-catcher*, I think.

"My mum says everyone gets disorganised when they have a new baby," Zuzanna says, which makes me feel better, then she spoils it by adding, "Although your baby is not that new any more, really."

I don't tell her about Uncle Clive or Lemmy. Even though she's my second-best friend, I don't think she'd understand. That is the trouble with a second-best friend, it's just not the same as a first-best friend.

This morning all the garibaldis left on the kitchen table had been eaten. Mum says she couldn't understand it as there was nearly a full packet

there last night; she said maybe Uncle
Clive got hungry in the night.

Anyway I have other things on my mind at
the moment. I need to find the second Allotment
Club poster as soon as we get to school. Gran was
very annoyed that Mum is taking Clover to dig up
the school field in the rain. She said Mum was, "Off
on one of her mad schemes again, which is all very
well but she needs to clean the bathroom one day."

I thought Gran was going to talk some sense
into Mum but all she did was end up volunteering
to look after Clover on Thursday so Mum doesn't
have to bring her with her, which has not helped at
all. Gran says she's only doing a couple of hours,
though, because she's not going to turn into one of
those "unpaid silver surfer child-minders". I don't
think anyone really knew what she was on about
but Mum seemed grateful enough.

I leave Zuzanna by the classroom door saying
I've got a note to hand in at the office and then I

slip off down the corridor to the Key Stage One noticeboard. I see the poster straight away and I can't believe how many people have signed up: loads of Year Ones and Twos! Luckily, there's no one around as everyone has gone into class and I am just reaching up to pull the poster down when—

"Ah, Emily, signing up for your mother's Allotment Club! What a splendid idea." I jump like a frightened frog as Mr Meakin appears from nowhere. He gives me a head-teacher-type slow nod. "Parents like yours are an asset to the school! And I'm very impressed that you are joining in. Too many young people don't support their parents' efforts."

I give him a weak smile and say, "Well . . . err," as usual.

"Carry on," he says.

He waits as I pick up the pen and slowly write "Emily Sparkes" at the bottom of the list.

"Jolly good," he says, "and I think that's quite enough members for the time being, don't you? I'll pass this on to your mother. I'm sure she'll be very pleased. Now, off to class."

And he pulls out the pins and turns and walks off with the poster flapping in his hand.

Disaster!

I am trying to worry but it is not easy to find the time as all morning we are doing Harvest stuff. Mrs Lovetofts is very excited about the Harvest Festival (it takes a very particular type of person to get excited about a Harvest Festival). First of all we have to go to the hall and practise singing "Oats and Beans and Barley Grow", with lots of actions.

Mrs Lovetofts is a very enthusiastic singer and she has a very high voice. It's OK, though, because she sings so loudly she can't hear that no one else is joining in. She does, however, notice that Alfie and Gross-Out are doing extra actions that "are not funny, not clever and definitely not in the song", and they have to sit out for the rest of the lesson.

Next we have to do the special school Harvest Festival song, which we do every year and it is very boring and very embarrassing. Someone brings something to put on the Harvest Table and everyone else has to sing about it while they do it. Last year I brought a marrow and had to carry it through the assembly hall while everyone sang:

Emily's brought a big green marrow
A big green marrow
A big green marrow
Emily's brought a big green marrow
To put on the Harvest Table

This year I'm definitely bringing something you can't sing about. I haven't worked out what that is yet, but it needs to have about twenty syllables.

We practise singing about "Joshua" and "some lovely white turnips" and "Nicole" and "some crusty brown rolls", then it all goes a bit wrong when Mrs Lovetofts starts a verse of "Amy-Lee's brought a big bag of sprouts" and Amy-Lee goes off in a big strop because she thinks she's being picked on. "No one likes sprouts," she says.

"Yeah," Yeah-Yeah Yasmin agrees.

Then we go back to the classroom and get to design Harvest Festival posters in groups. The best posters will go on the wall. My group is Chloe, Zuzanna,

Gross-Out Gavin and Alfie – and I am already thinking this is turning out to be a very bad morning before I happen to look out of the window and notice a familiar figure crossing the playground to the school field, pushing a Baby Eco-Jogger Deluxe buggy with one hand and carrying a spade in the other.

"Right, let's get this show on the road!" I say in such an enthusiastic way that everyone looks a bit worried, but at least it distracts them from looking out of the window.

Although Gross-Out is a total pain, he is surprisingly good at art, so we give him the task of drawing the pictures.

"What shall I draw?" he asks, which is quite a sensible question from him; his usual questions are things like "Guess what colour bogey I just got out of my nose?"

"Err, harvesty-type things . . . pumpkins?" I say.

"Pumpkins?" Chloe says. "It's Harvest, not Halloween."

"How about wheat sheaves and a loaf of bread?" Zuzanna says.

"Are you serious!" Chloe says. "Don't you know I have a wheat intolerance?"

"No you—"

I don't get to finish my sentence because Chloe shrieks, "OMG! That freaky person is totes digging up the field again!"

"I can't believe it. They've brought a baby with them," Zuzanna says. "It can't be very good for it to be out in the cold."

"Perhaps we should call ChildLine," Chloe says.

"CAN we just get on with the poster?" I say.

With all this going on, Alfie and Gross-Out have got bored and are trying to poke each other up the nose with the felt pens.

"Miss," Chloe says, "Gavin and Alfie are being disgusting," although really it would be more of a surprise if someone said, "Miss, Gavin and Alfie are *not* being disgusting." But Mrs Lovetofts decides

that they had better come and work near her so we are down to three.

"That's better anyway," Chloe says. "Don't worry, I will be the drawing person now because I am very good at art, unlike some people," she says looking at me. Chloe always says I can't draw, but I'm not that bad, especially if you want an alien, although I suppose that's not very harvesty either.

"OK, so, remembering that it is not Halloween and that pumpkins are totally out, and being careful not to upset people with allergies, what are we going to draw?" Chloe says.

"Sweetcorn," Zuzanna says, "or marrows, there are always loads of marrows at Harvest Festivals."

"That's because everyone grows them but no one likes them so they send them into school," I say, "and then they get packaged up with all the other stuff people don't want and sent to the old people, who have to eat them because they were a present. My mum says it's basically like composting."

"Your mum?" Chloe says suspiciously. "Is she into gardening then?"

"No, no – definitely not," I say, trying not to look towards the school field. "Like, if you say 'mud' to my mum she will go 'yuck' really loudly. Totally."

"Can we please hurry up and decide what to draw," Zuzanna says. "Everyone else has nearly finished."

"Steak," Chloe says, "and chips. Everybody likes steak and chips."

"Not if you're a vegetarian," Zuzanna says, who is, except for when her mum doesn't let her.

"You can't draw steak and chips for harvest," I say. "It doesn't grow."

"Oh duh!" Chloe says. "Like a cow doesn't grow, like potatoes don't grow."

"Yes, well, maybe but that's not the sort of thing they mean by harvest. It's got to be vegetables and stuff."

Chloe rolls her eyes. "Well, what about peas?"

"Peas?"

"Yes, they grow, they're vegetables . . . and I like peas."

"I suppose peas are OK, but it's usually more carrots and cabbages and stuff."

"Urrgh! I cannot stand any vegetables that begin with C."

"Look, Chloe, you don't have to like it, just draw it," I say.

"This is exactly why I'm an artist and you're not, Emily," Chloe says. "An artist doesn't paint things they don't like. You can so tell Vincent Van Gogh was in love with Mona Lisa."

"It was Leonardo da Vinci who painted the Mona Lisa," Zuzanna says.

"Yes, well, it was probably a love triangle," Chloe says.

I am beginning to think we will never get this poster done. I try a different suggestion. "Well, what about fruit? Apples?"

"Yuck!"

"Plums?"

"Errgh."

"Chloe, what fruit do you like?" asks Zuzanna.

"Raisins," Chloe says, "as long as they've got chocolate on."

Which is how we end up with a poster advertising the Harvest Festival decorated with peas and chocolate raisins and looking like it's got the sort of unpleasant rash your mum would put cream on.

At the end of the day Mrs Lovetofts announces the three posters that will go up around the school. Ours is not one of them. There is a lot of chatter and scraping of chairs as everyone leaves to go home. I am also about to leave but I notice Zuzanna is still sitting in her seat staring into space.

"What's up with her?" Chloe says.

"Are you OK, Zuzanna?" I ask.

Zuzanna doesn't blink but keeps staring at the wall. She says slowly, "This is the first time ever that a piece of work I have been involved with has not been the best in the class."

"Well," Chloe says, "I did say steak and chips but no one would listen."

I am about to point out that steak and chips do not feature heavily on the winning posters either when I notice my mum is heading back across the school field bouncing Clover along in the Baby Eco-Jogger Deluxe.

"I'm going to practise poster-making all evening," Zuzanna says, collecting up her pencil case. "Are you walking home, Emily?"

"No. Err, emergency. Sorry, got to go!" I say, grabbing my stuff and running out of the door.

I get outside just as Mum reaches the school door. "Hi, Mum," I say dragging her by the arm to get her away before Chloe and Zuzanna come out.

"Hey, what's the hurry?" she says.

"Come on, I'll miss my favourite programme."

"Favourite programme?" Mum says, trailing along behind.

"Yes, you know, *Dana Devene, Domestic Queen*. Starts at four o'clock."

"What, that silly woman who is always harping on about home-made pillowcases and lavender bags? Since when did you like that?"

Since it was the first thing that came into my head, I think, hurrying out of the school gate.

"I don't know anyone with a normal life who has time for decorating jam jars," Mum says, sounding out of breath, "and will you please stop walking so fast. It's not easy to keep up in these wellies."

I slow down to a normal speed. I don't think anyone from school will see us from here.

"Phew," Mum says, "you really do want to watch that programme, don't you?"

"Dana Devene is very creative," I say.

"Yes, well, I've been very creative myself today.

97

I've marked out the area for the new school allotment and I'm all ready to go with the first Allotment Club on Thursday. And I wanted to say thank you, Emily."

"Thank you?"

"Yes, for signing my poster. I am very lucky to have such a supportive daughter."

"Look, Mum, about that—"

"And to say thank you I was going to take you to Betty's Cafe for tea, but as you're in such a rush to get home—"

"Oh – no, I'm not, not really," I say.

"But what about *Dana Devene*?" Mum says as we come to a stop outside Betty's Cafe.

"Well, she's very creative," I say, "but Betty makes much better cheese toasties. Come on."

CHAPTER EIGHT

Mostly Mud

Thursday

It has now been three days since Uncle Clive moved in, which is definitely more than "a couple" and he still doesn't seem to be showing many signs of moving out again. Everyone in my house is in a bad mood. There seem to be bits of Uncle Clive everywhere. He has enormous boots which he leaves in the hall, making it very difficult to open the front door, and an oily-smelling leather jacket which he leaves hanging in different places like a big black bat. Wherever he sits, in the living room or the kitchen, he seems to take up most of the space and there's not much space to start off with. Also he has an awful lot of hair which always gets in the way when you're trying to watch TV.

I have been sleeping in with Clover (who Uncle Clive still calls Flora; he says it's a confusion caused by buttery spreads, so I suppose we should be grateful he doesn't call her Lurpak), which is rubbish because she wakes up when I go to bed (sorry, when I go to *camp* bed), so I can't sleep and she can't sleep, and then Mum has to try to get her off to sleep so she can't sleep and that wakes Dad up and then he can't sleep. In fact, the only person who *can* sleep is Uncle Clive, and you know he's asleep because you can hear him snoring.

I suppose it's not his fault though. He has to stay somewhere and he does try to be kind. Last night he gave me a KitKat he found in his jacket. It was a bit squashed but then so are most things he comes in contact with.

Mum says, "It wouldn't be so bad if he didn't keep slipping downstairs in the night to eat things. There are two Chelsea buns gone again this morning."

Chelsea buns? Since when did we have Chelsea buns? There are things that go on in this house that I have no idea about.

Today Uncle Clive is going to see Daisy to see if they can "work things out". Everyone has their fingers crossed.

I finish my Coco-Crispies while watching Dana Devene again. Today she is showing everyone how to arrange flowers in a Japanese style called ikebana. It is mostly fascinating because it is basically two flowers and a bit of twig but it looks really nice. It must be very good for people on a budget. Even my mum might like it if I called it Frugal Flowers. I should mention it to her – if we had some flowers in the house it wouldn't smell so much of nappies and motorbike oil.

I am just saying goodbye to Clover and crossing her fingers for Uncle Clive and Daisy to get back together when Mum comes in and gives me my packed lunch and another bag.

"Your wellies, love," she says. "Thank you so much for volunteering to be in the Allotment Club. I'll see you at lunchtime."

Oh no! I can't believe I forgot. Thursday already.

All morning I am wondering what I can do to get out of Allotment Club. I could try faking a mysterious illness but I did that last week to get out of choir practice and the week before to get out of country dancing, so I'm pretty sure it won't work again. My usual Emily Sparkes creativityness

has deserted me. I am doomed to a lunch hour of digging the field in ladybird wellies.

The buzzer goes for lunch and Mrs Lovetofts says, "Line up for hot dinners, please." Everyone rushes to line up; everyone has a hot dinner on Thursday because it's pizza. Everyone except me. I have got a packed lunch which I'm supposed to eat after Allotment Club.

I am just wondering if I could get away with putting red felt-pen spots on my face and saying I'm allergic to mud when I finally get a good idea. What if I just say I forgot? I'll take my packed lunch into the dining room with everyone else and pretend that Allotment Club totally slipped my mind. Mum won't be able to come and get me because she'll have all those little kids to look after. It might work. I feel a little bit guilty but really it's Mum's own fault for having rubbish ideas and anyway, anything is better than the ladybird wellies.

The little kids always get to go in for lunch earlier and as we walk down the corridor towards the dinner hall, they are all trooping back the other way. An alarming number of them are wearing wellies and are obviously on their way to Allotment Club next. I pretend not to notice them.

Just as we get to the door Mr Meakin comes out of his office. "Ah, lunch is it, ladies?" he says to Zuzanna, Chloe and me, to which the sensible answer would be, "Well, duh, what do you think?" but we just smile and say, "Yes, Sir."

"Well, let's hope the Key Stage Ones haven't eaten it all," he says with a little laugh. No one else laughs, though, because he says this so often he has totally worn all the laughing out of it.

"And you too, Emily?" he says. "Aren't you supposed to be helping your mother with Allot—"

"A LOT! Yes, Sir, I am helping my mother with A

LOT today. Just on my way now. Sorry, girls, got A LOT to do!" and I walk off in the other direction as quickly as possible, leaving Zuzanna and Chloe staring after me.

There is no hope now. I can't get out of it; I have to accept my fate. I go back to class and put on the wellies of doom and head out of the door.

I slip out into the playground and look around to make sure there is no one to see me, before sprinting (not easy in wellies) across the field to where my mother is surrounded by a whole army of over-excited Year Ones and Twos.

"Ah there you are, Emily, thank goodness," Mum says. "OK, everyone, quieten down please."

The little children calm down very slightly

as Mum says, "Right, everyone, there is a lot of weeding and digging to be done to make this into an allotment.

Today we are going to make a start on some digging for the vegetable plots so we can put in some seeds in the spring."

"But why can't we grow something now?" asks a little girl.

"Because it's autumn now, seeds grow in spring," Mum says.

"But why can't we get some autumn-growing seeds?" says another.

"Yeah, why can't we grow pumpkins for Halloween," says a little boy and all the little kids start joining in with "Pumpkins! Pumpkins!"

"Quiet, please!" Mum says a little more firmly than before. "Pumpkins won't grow in time."

"They do at Asda," he says.

"Now look," Mum says, "we have to dig the beds first."

"I want to grow a flower," says another little girl.

"These will be for vegetables," Mum says.

"I don't want to grow vegetables, I want to grow flowers," she says and starts to cry.

"Err ... don't cry," Mum says. "Look, let's do some digging, that'll be fun," and she quickly hands out the spades. Unfortunately, Mum has had to borrow the spades from Reception's sandpit and there are not enough to go round.

"Want a spade," says a little boy who doesn't have one.

"You have to share," Mum says.

The little boy folds his arms and sulks. "Weed," he says.

"No," Mum says, "dig. We don't have to worry about weeds yet, we just need to dig the vegetable beds."

"Flowers!" wails the little girl. "Want flowers." Mum kneels down to speak to her and she flings her arms round Mum's neck and refuses to let go, so Mum picks her up and she buries her snotty head in Mum's neck and blubs, "Want flowers."

"Weed," says the little boy again.

"Will you please stop talking about weeds," Mum says in the sort of voice that means she is about to say she needs a big lie-down.

"Weed," says the little boy and starts crying too.

"He means he's wet himself, Miss," says a little girl. "He always does."

"Great," Mum says, and for a moment I am afraid that she will do a big lie-down right there and then on the field but she just takes a deep breath and says, "Right. Emily, perhaps you could take these two back to class." She tries to put the flower girl down but she just hangs on tighter and wails, "Flowers."

"Weed," cries the little boy.

"Urrrgh!" Mum says. "OK, Emily, get the rest of them digging. I just need to take these two back to their teacher." And she takes the flower girl and the weed boy off, leaving me in charge of about a hundred (well, OK, eleven) five- and six-year-olds all armed with spades and definitely dangerous.

I don't even have time to shout after Mum, "I don't think this is a very good idea," because I have to go and rescue another little girl whose welly has come off in the mud. I am trying to get her welly back on before *she* starts crying but all the other kids are getting restless so I just sort of shout, "Get digging." I get the little girl's boot back on and now I have got muddy knees and muddy hands which I wipe off on my skirt and by the time I look around there are lots of little kids digging random holes everywhere. I don't think that's quite what Mum had in mind but once they've started it's difficult to get them to stop.

"Err . . . I think we're supposed to be digging in the same place," I say. "Like over here where Mum, I mean Miss, has marked out the bed." But it is no use. As soon as I get one kid to dig in the right place, another one wanders off and starts digging somewhere else.

"Look, can everyone stop digging a minute," I say.

"But you told us to start digging," says a little boy.

"Yeah, but now she said stop, stupid," says another little boy.

"I'm not stupid," says the first.

"Yes you are," says the other.

"Look," I shout, "just don't dig and don't argue for a minute." They all go quiet and I think I have just got things under control and, thank goodness, I can see Mum coming back when the second little boy mutters, "But he is stupid though."

"I am not!" says the first little boy and whacks the other on the leg with his spade.

"Owwww!" he shouts, and I am thinking, *Please don't start crying*, but then I wish he had because instead he picks up a lump of mud and throws it at the spade boy's face.

"No! Don't throw mud!" I say, which is obviously

totally the wrong thing to say because no one else had thought of it till then, but now they all seem to think it is a good idea. Within a couple of seconds there is mud flying everywhere, the children are slipping and sliding about and screeching with laughter. "Stop!" I shout. "Come on now. That's enough. Stop!"

"Emily!" Mum says, running back across the field. "You're supposed to be looking after them!" and a big ball of mud splats her right in the face.

"Enough!" yells Mum, once she has got the mud out of her mouth. "Allotment Club is over for today. Please go and wash your hands." The little kids troop off across the field back towards school and I think that hand washing is not going to make a lot of difference. Really, they all need hosing down.

"Sorry, Mum," I say as she collects up the spades.

"It's OK, Emily, it wasn't really your fault. I think they might be a bit young," she says with a sigh. "Perhaps I'll give them another go in spring, when they can plant some seeds."

Result!

"Does that mean you're not going to do any more Allotment Club this term, then?" I say.

"Oh no. I still need to get the veg plots dug. I need older children. I'll put another poster up on the Key Stage Two noticeboard. Do you think any of your friends would be interested?"

"Sorry, can't hear," I say, walking away quickly. "Think I've got mud in my ear."

CHAPTER NINE

Competition Calamity

Thursday - Still School

By the time I have managed to get most of the mud off it is nearly time for the bell and I haven't even eaten my lunch yet. I go into class to find Zuzanna and Chloe already there.

"There you are," Zuzanna says. "We've been looking everywhere for you."

"Yes, where have you been? And why are you

so . . . so yucks-ville?" Chloe says pulling a face at my muddy skirt.

I can't even begin to think of an excuse and also I am basically weak from hunger so I shove a limp tuna sandwich into my mouth to buy some time. Fortunately, while I am chewing, Mrs Lovetofts arrives, acting far too excited for a teacher.

"Emily, Emily!" she say flappily, "such exciting news, I don't know where to start!" She clasps her hands together and sort of bounces up and down on the spot.

"Err . . . yeth, Mith?" I say through my thandwich, I mean, sandwich.

"The poem! The competition! The Mum in a Million!" she says.

The mad teacher, I think.

"Your mum is . . . a finalist! I got an email just now. There are three lucky finalists, and your mum is one of them!" She gives herself a little hug.

A finalist. My mum? This doesn't make sense. "But she can't be, I mean . . . she's not very good at mum stuff."

"Of course she is, Emily! You said so, she bakes and cleans and sews – marvellous. She's a supermum!"

"But . . ." I am finding it hard to take all this in and even Chloe and Zuzanna have stopped talking and are just sort of staring.

"Look!" Mrs Lovetofts waves a piece of paper at me. "Here's the email."

I read it out.

Dear Emily,

Thank you for entering your mum into Mum in a Million!

We really loved your poem and I'm delighted to tell you that your mum has been chosen as one of the three finalists!

We will be contacting you later in the week to arrange a surprise visit for your mum from none other than A-list Celebrity Superwoman Dana Devene!

We will be in touch soon with further details.

Congratulations!!

The Dana Devene Domestic Queen Team

Before I even have time to react, Chloe has recovered enough to snatch the email out of my hand. "A-list!" she says. "Like where? Outer Mongolia?"

Mrs Lovetofts ignores her and continues, "I gave them a call and they have confirmed some of the details. Dana Devene is going to do a special broadcast from the homes of each of the finalists. She will be coming to your house to interview your

116

mum and find out all about her. You must be so excited!"

"Err ... I'm not sure what Mum will say," I say, thinking I have a pretty good idea of what she will say, something like – *I haven't got time to talk to that silly embroidered-cushion woman.*

"But that's just it, Emily. It's all hush-hush. The mums don't get to know until Dana turns up on their doorstep with a big bunch of flowers!"

"Umm." I am trying to think quickly but my brain is not working very well. It has probably been completely affected by Uncle Clive's oil fumes. "On the doorstep . . . of our house?"

"Yes, though I wonder if Dana might pop into the school too, seeing as the entry came through us? And your mum is doing the Allotment Club here—"

Chloe makes a sort of squeaky sound.

"I mean, she's practically a member of staff. Look, she's out there now." Before I can stop her Mrs Lovetofts points out of the window and waves at my mum.

"OMG!" Chloe says, finding her voice. "I knew that gardener man looked familiar."

"It's a *she*, Chloe," I say. "My mum isn't a man."

"May as well be in that jumper," Chloe says, wrinkling up her nose.

Mrs Lovetofts is still talking. "Yes, I'm sure Dana would like to pay us a visit. Oh, she'll love the cross-stitch bookmarks we made, so shabby chic!"

Well, I think, *mine's definitely shabby*. I have never seen Mrs Lovetofts like this before, she's a bit . . . starstruck.

"So what happens now, Mrs Lovetofts? Mrs Lovetofts?"

She is gazing dreamily across the classroom.

"Oh yes, sorry, just wondering what to wear for

the big day. Next *Dana's people* will talk to *your people*," she says.

"People? I don't have people."

"I mean a responsible adult. Your dad."

I don't think anyone who keeps copper pipes in his living room can really be classed as responsible but as usual I just manage to say, "Err . . ."

"Good, I'll pass on your home number and as long as he agrees then your mum's special surprise will be ready to go! What absolute fun!" Mrs Lovetofts continues, "Just imagine, she could win the star prize, a complete makeover."

And now I am beginning to get more than a bit worried. I mean, they can't really come round, my mum is probably more likely to win Domestic Disaster in a Million. "But what if my mum doesn't want to be in the competition, Mrs Lovetofts? I'm not sure a complete makeover is her type of thing."

"Oh, Emily, of course it is, all mums like a bit of pampering."

"Yes, but what if things aren't quite what Dana and her, err, people, expect when they arrive?"

"Don't worry so much, Emily, it will be fine. As long as you don't have rats or something," she laughs.

"Lemmy!" I say.

"Pardon?" Mrs Lovetofts says.

"Err . . . *lummy*," I say. "It's what my gran says . . . sometimes."

Mrs Lovetofts looks a little concerned. "Perhaps you need to have a little rest now, Emily, it's all been very exciting," and she bustles out of the room.

"I am still in total shocks-ville," Chloe says. "That scarecrow person is your mum?"

"She's doing a project for Mr Meakin," I say.

"She must really like mud," Zuzanna says, looking out of the window.

"But now you have done, like, a double lie,

Emily," Chloe says. "It's bad enough lying in your homework but lying to win a competition is really bad."

"It wasn't a lie, it was a mistake!" I say.

"I think Chloe has a point, though," Zuzanna says. "I mean, no offence, Emily, but there is no way your mum is going to win."

"Yes, in fact I wouldn't be surprised if you don't get arrested for making a false claim in your competition entry," Chloe says.

"Can you get arrested for that?" I ask, finding another thing to worry about when I am already full up with worrying.

"I expect so," said Chloe. "They can't just let people go around cheating all the time, can they?"

CHAPTER TEN

How Do You Make a Perfect Mum?

Thursday – Home

I get home and I nearly have to bash the front door down to get it open because Mum has left her muddy wellies on top of Uncle Clive's motorbike boots in the hall. And I am thinking, *If Uncle Clive's motorbike boots are here that means his feet are*

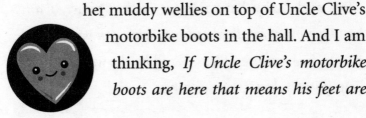

123

here too, which means they did not stay at Daisy's,
and so neither did he.

I know I am right when I get into the kitchen to
find Mum, Uncle Clive and his feet sitting round
the table. Clover is on Mum's knee looking very
bored, probably sick of hearing about motorbikes.
Uncle Clive and Mum are drinking tea again and
paying absolutely no attention to the bin that
needs emptying or the cereal bowls from this
morning that still haven't found their way into the
dishwasher. Once you know Dana Devene is going
to be filming your kitchen you see it all a lot more
clearly, and it is clearly a right mess.

Uncle Clive is looking very glum and Mum looks
at me and gives a little shake of her head. This is
very clever Mum sign language which means: *Uncle*
Clive and Daisy have not got back together, I am
having a bit of a talk about it to him, can you go and
give us five minutes, please. And by the way, it might
help if you take Clover with you.

I wish I was as good at sign language as Mum is, as I would like to say back, *How many more rooms in this house am I going to be kicked out of because Uncle Clive can't keep a girlfriend? And by the way can I have a chocolate mini roll?*

But I just make a huffy sound, pick up Clover and take her into the living room. I carefully step

 over the copper pipes and scoot around the clothes airer before taking Clover upstairs for a chat.

I have a quick peep into my room on the way past to see if I still recognise it. To be fair, it is not too messy. In fact, it is a lot tidier than it usually is, although that stack of *Bike Mechanic* magazines is never going to look right balanced on top of my old dolls' house. Funny, though, my bookshelves seem to have disappeared, and some of the boxes of old toys. I supposed they've been moved to make room for Uncle Clive; he does take up a lot of space. I just wish I could have my room back. I

mean, what if Uncle Clive and Daisy never get back together?

We go into Clover's room and sit on the camp bed. Well, I sit and Clover lies on her back and wishes she could sit.

"OK, Clover, I need some advice. Mum is going to be on TV as a Mum in a Million, and when she does I'll get arrested for fraud or something because she is *so* not."

"Da," says Clover, which is another new word, although not really very helpful.

"She needs to be able to sew and bake."

"Da," says Clover.

"And she's even supposed to look nice."

"Daaaaaa," says Clover, surprisingly loudly, and then she does a burp and looks a bit startled.

I hear Uncle Clive's heavy steps as he comes upstairs and goes into my room and shuts the door.

"Come on, Clover," I say. "I think this is definitely time for a chocolate mini roll."

When I get downstairs Mum has gone off down the shed again. I don't know what she finds to do in there all the time. I put Clover in her bouncy baby seat, and as I have been left in charge of a tiny infant when I am not much more than a child myself I decide to have two chocolate mini rolls to give me energy. Unfortunately Lemmy seems to have got there first and there are only a few crumbs left in the box. That rat really does have to go. I have a crawl around the kitchen to look for him but I don't spot him anywhere, although once I think I see a little pink eye peeping out from behind the bread bin, but when I look there's nothing there.

Luckily Dad gets home. I tell him Mum has gone to hide in the shed and he's in charge of Clover, as he is an actual parent, and I have important computer stuff to do, which is mostly talking to Bella.

Emily says: BELLA!!!! Totes disaster!

 Bella says: Totes?

 Emily says: Sorry, it's because Chloe's back.

 Bella says: So, what's up?

 Emily says: That poem you made me write?

 Bella says: Poem?

 Emily says: Well, that perfect mum list, I accidentally turned it into a poem and Mrs Lovetofts entered it into a competition and now I've got an email.

 Bella says: You lost me at "totes".

Emily says: My mum has been
shortlisted in the Mum in a
Million competition!

 Bella says: Well . . . that's
good, isn't it?

 Emily says: No because it's
all a lie. She is totally
not a Mum in a Million - she
probably isn't even a Mum in a
Few.

 Bella says: Don't be mean. I
think she's nice.

 Emily says: Being nice is not
a category. She needs to be
able to bake, sew and clean.

 Bella says: Eww. How does that
make you a good mum? Whatever

happened to being kind and
funny?

 Emily says: Look, I don't
make the rules. I might get
arrested for competition fraud
or something. What am I going
to do?

 Bella says: Can I get back to
you on that? It's milking time.

I think she is being much less helpful these days.

I can see the only way out of this is going to be
with some Emily Sparkes creativityness – trouble
is, I'm not sure I've got enough left. I think I need
to sleep on it.

CHAPTER ELEVEN

Calamity Upon Calamity

Friday

I didn't get to sleep on it very much, even with my head under the pillow I could still hear Uncle Clive snoring. I get up early and creep out of the room so that I don't wake Clover. I need to watch breakfast TV and see what's happening with the competition. Sure enough, before I can even get around to finding out if Lemmy has eaten the

Coco-Crispies, Dana Devene's big smiley face appears.

"Good morning, all you fabulous mums out there, and a particularly good morning to three special ladies who are the finalists in our Mum in a Million Competition. You don't know who you are yet, but let me assure you, we do, and on Tuesday, Wednesday and Thursday morning next week we will be popping up on the doorstep of our lovely mums' homes to see why they are so special."

I don't care if Lemmy has had all the Coco-Crispies, because I can't face them now anyway. It's really true, Dana Devene is going to come to our house. I turn the TV off because seeing Dana Devene grinning all the time is making me feel ill.

I put Wavey Cat on top of the TV and flick his paw. "I need help!" I say. "I have to get Mum out of this competition. You're my last hope. Bella is obsessed with goats and all

Clover says is 'da'." Wavey Cat waves gently at me and as I watch I think, *hang on a minute . . . da . . . dad . . . DAD!* Clover was right all along. Thank you, Wavey Cat! Of course, they have to have Dad's permission. All I have to do is get Dad to say no, then they'll have to disqualify Mum and get someone else. Oh, what a relief!

I can hear Dad moving around upstairs. Once he gets downstairs he will only be around for ten minutes to make a cup of tea and have some cornflakes before he goes to work. I need to act fast.

"Dad," I say as he walks into the living room, "there's this thing they're doing at school. Some of the kids are making a pretend TV programme and they want to go round and film at some people's houses, but they have to get your permission."

"Huh?" Dad says, only half awake.

"If someone phones up and says they want to

come round and film, will you say no, please? Because I don't want to do it."

"Don't want to do what?" he says vacantly, ambling into the kitchen.

"Make a film. Look if anyone phones and asks your permission—"

"Hey! Someone's eaten all the cornflakes!" Dad says.

"Dad, listen, if someone phones you—"

"S'pose I'll have to have toast."

"Dad—"

"Oh for goodness' sake, the bread's all gone too."

"You have to say no!" I shout.

"OK, Emily, I get it. If anyone phones for permission to do anything I say no," he snaps. "Now I'm going to work. Hungry."

Well, I think that worked.

At school Mrs Lovetofts is getting very excited about the Harvest Festival, which is next Thursday.

"Thank your parents for all the contributions so far. Please tell them we have enough courgettes and marrows now, but we are still open to other contributions. A cake or some fruit, maybe?"

"My mum says she's got a tin of pears you can have that's nearly out of date," Gross-Out says.

"Very thoughtful," Mrs Lovetofts says. "Now, we might be getting a rather exciting visitor next week so I want to make sure the classroom looks tip-top."

She beams brightly at me and I think, *Very sorry to disappoint you, Mrs Lovetofts, but the visitor will be going elsewhere.*

During first break Mrs Lovetofts asks for volunteers to sharpen the pencils. "We don't want Ms Devene to ask to borrow a pencil and find it broken, do we? Imagine the embarrassment!" she says.

Zuzanna and I volunteer, Zuzanna because she always volunteers for everything, and me because she is my second-best friend and it's better than being stuck with Chloe all breaktime going on about what colour Jessie J paints her toenails.

Unfortunately, even though Chloe has not volunteered, she decides to stay in anyway and watch us volunteering.

"You must be totes stressed about getting arrested, Emily," she says when Mrs Lovetofts has gone out. "But jail is probably not as bad as people make out and you will be bound to get out early as it is your first crime. It is, isn't it?"

"Don't worry, Chloe, it's all sorted. I have withdrawn my mum from the competition."

Chloe looks very disappointed. "But that means you won't get arrested?"

"No." I smile confidently. "I won't."

"What a super job, girls!" Mrs Lovetofts says, bustling back into the room, and I wonder if anyone has ever not done a "super job" for Mrs Lovetofts. Somehow I don't think so.

"I just had a lovely chat to one of Ms Devene's people, Emily," she says. "They've spoken to your dad and it's all arranged! You're last on the list so they'll be coming round next Thursday morning. How exciting!"

What?!

"But they can't have spoken to him yet, he's at work," I say, with my head feeling definitely dizzyish.

"Well, they said they did. They called your house and spoke to Mr Sparkes and asked him for permission to come and film."

"But he must have said *no*. He promised, err, I mean, he said we were too busy."

"He must have had second thoughts. Apparently he said, 'Yeah, that all sounds cool. I guess.' Which gave them a little giggle, I understand."

I am totally confused. That doesn't sound like

Dad at all and anyway he's at work. In fact, it sounds a bit like ... Uncle Clive! Oh no! Uncle Clive is Mr Sparkes too.

"But that was my uncle—"

"They also told me about the lovely children's prize that's on offer."

"Children's prize?" Chloe says.

"Yes. An exciting shopping or museum trip to London for the winner and two friends. Doesn't that sound fantastic?"

"Yes, that all sounds great but—"

"It sounds totes amazeballs, Mrs Lovetofts," Chloe says before I can stop her. "As you say, all mums love a bit of pampering and Emily's mum could definitely use the makeover more than most."

"Wonderful," Mrs Lovetofts says. "I must say, this is almost more exciting than the Harvest Festival. What a week!" And she hurries off again.

"Chloe! What did you go and say that for? My mum is so totally not a Mum in a Million. What am I going to do when Dana Devene comes knocking on the door? I don't know who is going to be more shocked, my mum because she's in the competition, or Dana when she gets a look at the state of our kitchen."

"Don't worry, Emily. Zuzanna and I will help you out."

"Will we?" Zuzanna says.

"Help me with what? How?"

"Fix up your mum. Make her win."

"I really don't think that's possible," Zuzanna says, shaking her head.

"You are taking a very negative attitude here, Zuzanna," Chloe says.

"You haven't actually been inside Emily's house, have you, Chloe?" Zuzanna says.

"No, but really, how bad can it be?"

Zuzanna and I exchange looks, but Chloe won't be put off. "Girls! Do you or do you not want to get an all-expenses-paid shopping trip to London?"

"I'd rather go to the museum," Zuzanna says.

"Well, we can discuss that later," Chloe says. "And don't forget we also get to meet an A-list celebrity!"

"I thought you said she was D-list?" I say.

"I'm having a reassessment. And let's face it, even a D-lister's a celeb round here. Of course, if she came to Mag Hall no one would give her a second glance."

"But we're never going to win," I say.

"No more negativity," Chloe says. "It's bouncing off me like a . . . boingy thing on a trampoline."

"But—"

"Boing!" Chloe says, putting her hands over her ears.

I sigh. "So what's the plan then?"

Chloe beams. "Zuzanna and I can come round on Sunday morning and we can *all* make a plan together. I mean, all we've got to do is teach your mum to cook, sew and look nice. How hard can it be?"

Everyone turns to look out of the window where my mum is leaning on her spade. I have a sort of sinking feeling in my tummy.

"In a week?" Zuzanna says.

"Yes," Chloe says. "Emily, we have a week to make your mum perfect!"

CHAPTER TWELVE

Fail to Plan, Plan to Fail

Sunday

It is Sunday. The day of the plan. I spent yesterday trying to think of ways to sort out the Mum in a Million disaster. The only things I came up with were:

a) get a new mum or,

b) move to Australia.

Neither of which are very likely to happen by Thursday.

Uncle Clive said he did take a phone call. He thought they were asking him if he wanted to be in a competition to win his mum a complete makeover. I don't think he can hear that well with all that hair hanging around his ears.

At least Zuzanna and Chloe are coming over at half past ten and surely three heads are better than one, even when one of them is Chloe's.

Mum says she's sorry I don't have my own room to go and sit in with my friends and we'll have to go in the kitchen, although I'm not sure if that means she's sorry for me or sorry she has to put up with us. I am not happy with the kitchen idea, though, because at any moment Lemmy could make an appearance, and anyway it is very difficult to make a secret plan in the middle of the kitchen on a Sunday morning. So Mum agrees we can go and sit in Clover's room. At least that's one thing

sorted out. There are a lot of things to be stressed about when your friends are coming round, like do you have anything to offer them to drink apart from Basics orange squash, and can you trust your dad not to call you his "little fairy elephant" or something. Luckily, Uncle Clive bought a bottle of Coke yesterday and Dad has gone to football. But never fear, there are a thousand other things to be embarrassed about so I won't miss out.

At exactly 10.30 the doorbell rings. Zuzanna must be in charge of timing.

I have to pick up Uncle Clive's boots before I can open the door.

"Seriously, Zuzanna, it can't be that bad," Chloe is saying as I answer the door.

"Hi, girls," I say.

"Ewwwww!" Chloe shrieks, pointing to Uncle Clive's boots. "What are those?"

"My uncle Clive's boots," I say trying to find somewhere to put them down that won't block the entire hall.

"They look like they belong to Hagrid," Zuzanna says with a nervous laugh.

"Yeees. I haven't really told you about Uncle Clive, have I?" I say, looking down at the boots in my hands and at a little pair of pink eyes staring up from one of them.

"Lemmy!" I hiss.

"What?" Chloe says.

"Err ... lemmy ... let me take you through to the living room," I say, hastily dumping the boots and Lemmy on top of the Baby Eco-Jogger Deluxe and dragging Chloe and Zuzanna down the hall.

"OMG!" Chloe says as we get to the living room. "What is with the pipes in the middle of the room?"

"Modern sculpture," I say. "It's very fashionable,

surprised you don't have one in your house. Shall we go upstairs?"

"Hello, Chloe," Mum says, carrying Clover into the room. "I thought that 'ewwwww' must be coming from you."

"Hi, Mrs Sparkes," Zuzanna says quickly. "Thanks for letting us come round."

"Hi, Zuzanna. Make yourselves at home, girls. Clover and I are going down to the shed." Mum smiles.

"The shed?" Chloe says. "Why would you do that? I thought sheds were for old men and lawnmowers and stuff like that."

"I have a little project I'm working on," Mum says as she heads for the back door.

"Seriously," Chloe says, "I'm beginning to think this is going to be totes hard work."

We go to sit in Clover's bedroom. On the way past I try to peep into my room as usual but the door is shut tight, like it's not even mine any more. In

Clover's room, Chloe and Zuzanna sit on the camp bed because they are the guests and I lean against the changing table, and I am very grateful that Mum has at least managed to empty the bin so that it doesn't smell really badly of nappies like it usually does.

"Don't you think sharing a room with a baby is like so . . . babyish?" Chloe says. "I'd hate it. Luckily, I have my own room, I mean rooms."

"It's only for a few days, Chloe," I say, but I'm not sure I believe that's true.

Chloe is in charge of writing and pens, and also deciding what gets written by the pens. So after about an hour all we have managed to come up with is:

<u>The Plan</u>
By Chloe, Zuzanna and Emily

★ Make a plan
★ Someone teach Emily's mum to sew something

★ Someone teach Emily's mum to bake a cake

★ Someone sort out Emily's mum's clothes and hair

"I really think we might need a bit more detail in this plan," Zuzanna says.

"What do you mean?" Chloe says. "That's about it. Well, that and get the house tidied up a bit. I'll put that in if you like." And she scribbles on the top of the paper.

"But who is going to do all these things?" I say. "Like baking a cake. We can't do it. We didn't exactly make a very good job of it last time we tried."

"We could always get one from Betty's and say she made it," Chloe says.

"No!" Zuzanna and I shout at the same time.

"That really didn't work out very well the last time, did it, Chloe?"

"Oh, no, I suppose not. We lost the baking competition. That was so unfair," Chloe says, looking as if she might be about to have a big sulk.

"Anyway," I say, "I don't want to say anything else that isn't true. I've already got in enough trouble by—"

"Making stuff up," Chloe says.

"– being creative," I say.

"And what about sewing?" Zuzanna says. "Who's going to teach her how to do that?"

There's a pause while everyone tries to think of a bit more plan. Then Chloe throws down the pen and paper.

"You two are so hung up on details. Something will turn up. You know, 'One Way or Another', as Olly Murs says."

"That's not Olly Murs, it's One Direction," says Zuzanna.

"He let them sing it," Chloe says. "He's very generous."

There is a small tap on the door. "I think you'll find that's a very old song by Blondie," says a gruff voice. Uncle Clive fills the doorway. "You young people need to learn where your music comes from."

And I think, *Just learning where my food comes from is causing me enough problems for one week, thank you.*

Uncle Clive gives a low chuckle and steps into the room. He carefully places a tray on the floor in front of us. Zuzanna and Chloe just stare, open-mouthed.

"Now then," he smiles, "I have to apologise for taking over young Emily's room so I have brought you some hot chocolate and some of my home-made chocolate brownies."

"You made these?" I say picking up a warm gooey brownie. "They're great."

"I do rather like a bit of baking," Uncle Clive says proudly. "Not as much as motorbike maintenance but a close second. Enjoy." He goes out, closing the door behind him.

"Who. Was. That?" Zuzanna whispers, looking a little pale.

"Don't worry," I say, "it's Uncle Clive. He's quite harmless, just a bit . . . big."

After about another half an hour of thinking we have no more plans and no more brownies.

"Perhaps we should just make a start on the first bit of the plan," I say. "You know, tidying up."

"OMG is that the time?" Chloe says, jumping to her feet. "I totes can't stay any longer. We are having a new home cinema installed and I don't want to miss the first screening."

"Home cinema? This is the first time you've mentioned it," I say.

"Well, you know me," Chloe says. "I hate to show off."

"I'm really sorry but I have to go now, too," Zuzanna says. "I don't want to be late for *X Factor*."

"But it isn't on for another seven hours," I say.

"Sorry, Emily, but I don't want to take any chances. The NV Boyz are in the danger zone tonight and I need to go round all my neighbours to get them to vote."

"But what about the plan?" I say.

"We have done quite a lot for you already," Chloe says, handing me the paper. "I'm sure you can finish off the last bit on your own."

I walk Zuzanna and Chloe to the front door. Zuzanna is a bit worried about bumping into Uncle Clive but we manage to get there without incident.

"Bye, Emily. Good luck," says Zuzanna as they head off down the path.

"Yep – and don't worry about thanking us now, you can do it when we go shopping in London," Chloe says.

"I want to go to the museum," Zuzanna says.

I shut the door.

I am left holding the plan:

The Plan - 2
By Chloe, Zuzanna and Emily

★ Make a plan ✔
★ Tidy up house
★ Vote for the NV Boyz on X factor

(When did Zuzanna write that in?)

★ Someone teach Emily's
mum to sew something
★ Someone teach Emily's
mum to bake a cake
★ Someone sort out
Emily's mum's clothes
and hair

I am not sure it is much of a plan. Mostly it is a list of difficult things to do, and it seems to be me who's doing them all.

I decide I'd better make a start. Tidying up. This would definitely be a lot easier if Gran came round to help but she never comes round on Sundays because it's her "Pie and Pilates" Club at the Community Hall. As usual it is down to me to sort everything out.

Uncle Clive is making strange grunty noises in the kitchen, so I go to see what is going on, but he is just trying to get his boots on. I don't know why he doesn't get some normal shoes. I'm sure his life would be easier.

"I'm going round to see Daisy," he says. "But I expect I'll be back later," he adds with a sigh.

"Have you caught Lemmy yet?" I ask.

"No, sorry. He jumped out of my boot and bolted under the tumble dryer. He does seem to like it here."

Once Uncle Clive has left the kitchen I can see what a mess it really is. Uncle Clive may be good at making cakes but he is not very good at clearing up after he's done it. There are bowls and cake tins, spilled flour and sticky cake  mixture all over the worktop, on top of the general muddle that is our kitchen. I'm not really sure where to start. I pick up a bag of sugar and open the cupboard to put it away.

"Eeek!" I shout as Lemmy comes leaping out from behind a box of teabags. I drop the sugar all over the floor just as Mum comes in. She seems to be all spattered with paint but I don't have time to wonder about that as Lemmy shoots across the floor and behind the cooker.

"What on earth?!" Mum says.

"It's just Lem—" I start to say, but then I realise she hasn't even noticed Lemmy, she is just looking round the kitchen.

"Oh, Emily," she says with a sigh. "What a mess you've made."

"But it wasn't—"

"Yoohoo!" calls Gran. "Clive just let me in. 'Pie and Pilates' was cancelled. Mrs Thorndyke got us double-booked with the carpet bowls club. Oh my glory days! What on earth has happened in here? Looks like I came round just in time. Emily," she says, shrugging off her coat, "pass me the Marigolds."

CHAPTER THIRTEEN

{ Sew Much to Do }

Monday

The good thing about Gran turning up was that she cleaned the kitchen from top to bottom. She said it was a better workout than Pilates, which is mostly sitting down anyway. The bad thing was she made me help, but never mind, at least we now have a sparkly clean kitchen for Dana to look at. That is, if I can keep it clean till Thursday.

Mum did not help. Gran let her off to do her shed project. I think it is very unfair but you don't want to argue with my gran or she'll give you a piece of her mind, which is never pleasant.

Gran stayed for dinner, which Mum made in an extremely tidy way; she clearly doesn't want a piece of Gran's mind either. I was going to message Bella but Gran decided to tell me all about her next-door neighbour's hedge. She is annoyed because it "keeps growing". I thought, *Yes, that is because it is a hedge not a fence.* I got so desperate I even offered to help Mum with the dinner, but she said dinner was all under control and she was super exceptionally busy. Then she sent me out of the kitchen, but not before I noticed she was

 doing something with a staple gun. I tried asking Dad what Mum was doing with a staple gun but he just said, "Eh?", which means he hadn't noticed. He is totally unobservant.

It took him three months to notice that we had a new lampshade in the hall.

We had frozen chicken kievs for dinner, although when we ate them they were cooked, obviously – even my mum is not that bad. And there were frozen (see previous note) chips and peas too, but totally nothing that had staples in. Curious.

But the most excellent thing that did happen last night is that Dad moved the copper pipes! Gran told him that the police have arrested some men on top of a church (I don't think they actually arrested them until they came down) and that the "danger has passed"; she is part of the Neighbourhood Watch team and is always finding out stuff from the police. Dad locked the copper pipes in the garage with a new extra-secure lock. I was so pleased I did twirls around the middle of the living room until I got told off for getting in the way of the *Strictly* results.

This morning Dana Devene is on TV again, getting very excited about meeting all the best mums in the country (plus mine). She is showing all the watching parents (mine are still in bed) how to make healthy and attractive packed lunches that children will actually want to eat. She has made a jewel-coloured salad and home-baked cheese straws with Moroccan hummus and fresh strawberry chocolate swirl cups. Apparently she does stuff like this every morning and only has to get up two hours early to do it.

I am just making notes on how to bake the perfect lunchbox mini cookies when Mum comes in wearing her dressing gown with the ripped pocket and carrying Clover, who looks much sweeter than she smells.

"What's in my packed lunch today, Mum?" I say.

"Err ... Marmite or tuna?" she says as she goes into the kitchen. "Oh hang on. I don't believe it. Someone's eaten all the bread again. You'll have to have a hot dinner." This is a conversation that would never happen in Dana Devene's house.

I could suggest Mum bakes up a few cheese straws but I don't think I'll get a positive response. To be fair, though, I'm not sure which school Dana Devene's kids go to because if you turned up at our school with jewel salad and hummus, people would think you had special dietary requirements.

I'm glad when it's time to go to school. Dad's extra-secure lock on the garage is so secure he can't open it. He is stomping about with a tin of WD-40 and a scowly face.

Mr Bevan-at-number-thirty-seven has called three times already to see why he's late to fit his new shower. Mum said Dad had better not answer his mobile for a bit because customers don't like being sworn at.

Zuzanna is smiling right off the scale when I get to her house. "Wasn't it fantastic?" she says.

I know I am supposed to know what she's talking about but most of my brain is being used up thinking about the next bit of the plan – getting Mum to sew.

"Err, yes, fantastic," I say.

"You did watch it, didn't you? You *did* vote?"

"Oh, for the NV Boyz. Yes, of course, they were brilliant." And I am hoping she will change the subject because I will probably say the wrong thing. Gran insisted we watch *Strictly Come Dancing*. She's gone right off *X Factor* since Brenda Belter went out after embarrassing herself in a Katy Perry dance routine.

Fortunately, Zuzanna is quite happy to do all the talking herself, with me just occasionally going "Wow" and "Ooh", which gives me plenty of time to think about how I am going to get Mum to learn to sew. Unfortunately, even though I have thought all the way to school, I haven't come up with anything.

Mrs Lovetofts is already in class when we get there. She is pinning up artwork and topic work and has even put up the raisin and peas Harvest Festival poster, although you can't really see it behind the stationery cupboard door. She has pinned up stuff everywhere. Also there are red and white checked curtains in the windows and matching frilly cushions in the book corner. The classroom looks like a cross between an art gallery and the Sylvanian Family treehouse.

"Do you think Dana will like it?" she says. "I've been working all weekend. I'm just wondering if we need some scented candles on the Tudor History table, you know, in front of that picture of Anne Boleyn getting beheaded. Just to soften it a bit?"

All day at school Chloe is talking about what she's going to buy in London when we go on our trip. Zuzanna is going on about exhibitions at the Science Museum and Mrs Lovetofts is polishing everything that doesn't actually run away. She even chased after Gross-Out Gavin with her duster.

Everyone is completely excited. And I am completely stressed. If I don't get this right, no one will be speaking to me for weeks. I bet I won't even get any prison visits.

I have been thinking very hard all day and I haven't come up with one idea to get my mum to sew, bake and dress nicely by precisely Thursday morning. I have to at least do the sewing task tonight. How am I going to get her to sew anything? My mum only ever really sews buttons on, and she's only done that since my dad had a serious clothing malfunction that time he went up a ladder but his trousers didn't.

I am just having an extra big worry when I see the cross-stitch bookmarks and I start to have an idea.

After class Mum is waiting to walk home again. I walk out and then I say, "Oops, I forgot my lunch box," in a very convincing way. I think I might be an actor when I grow up but now is not a good time to be making career decisions. I go back into class and everyone has gone but the cross-stitch box is still there. There is some thread, mostly sparkly orange and some muddy brown and lots of bookmarks that haven't had any sewing on them yet. I quickly snatch two bookmarks, two fat needles and a handful of thread and stick them in my coat pocket before heading back out to Mum. I think it is not really stealing, it's more like extra homework.

"Where's your lunchbox?" she says as I reach her.

"Silly me, I forgot, I had a hot dinner today," I say with an innocent smile and she rolls her eyes at me and we set off home.

 "Mum," I say after tea (gloopy-type pasta bake with extra courgettes), "can you help me with my homework?"

This is a sure-fire winner. No matter how busy she is, Mum always says yes to this question. Quite often she's not actually much help but she still feels too guilty to say no.

"OK, sweetheart," she says in her nice, patient Mum voice (this must be where I get my acting skills from). "How can I help?"

"I have to do a cross-stitch bookmark thing and I don't really know what to do."

"Cross stitch. Urrgh!" Mum says, which isn't very encouraging.

"It's quite fun really. Look," I say, producing the needles, thread and bookmarks. "I need to cross-stitch a flower ... maybe you could show me what to do using this one."

Mum looks extremely doubtful but she picks up the needle and thread and says, "Well, I haven't

168

done this since school but I think you just sort of sew in cross shapes." She begins to sew with sparkly orange thread. "Like this."

"Thanks," I say, "but how do you get it to look like a flower?"

Before long Mum is stitching away and has produced a rather wonky sparkly orange and muddy brown bookmark. It doesn't look like a flower, but it does look quite a lot like a giraffe with one leg, which is even more clever really.

It is lucky that we finish in time before Dad gets in because he is in a very bad mood. Someone stole the copper pipes out of his van when it was parked outside Mr Bevan-at-number-thirty-seven's. He stomps about saying, "I don't know what the world is coming to" and "You can't trust anyone nowadays" and other things that sound like Gran, and also some words that I only usually hear when Gran's driving.

Mum has saved him some pasta bake but she looks a bit worried and says, "I think I'd better go and defrost a steak."

Gran phones up and says Dad needs to be careful because she's heard "from her sources" that some copper pipes have been stolen from outside Mr Bevan-at-number-thirty-seven's. I tell her I'll let him know.

I am very sorry about Dad's pipes but I can't get upset because I am totally full up with being relieved. I have done another bit of the plan. Mum has done some sewing. I run upstairs and pull the plan out from my school bag.

The Plan – ~~2~~ 3
By Chloe, Zuzanna and Emily

★ Make a plan ✓
★ Tidy up house ✓
★ Vote for the NV Boyz on X factor ✓

(I know I forgot to do this but just in case Zuzanna looks)

★ ~~Someone~~ Emily teach Emily's mum to sew something ✓
★ Someone teach Emily's mum to bake a cake
★ Someone sort out Emily's mum's clothes and hair

OK. I know it's not the greatest sewing in the world but at least they can't say I lied.

CHAPTER FOURTEEN

Fantastically Fancy Fabrics

Tuesday

I wake up, and it is today – and today is the day the first finalist gets interviewed on breakfast TV. I slip quietly downstairs and get myself a bowl of Coco-Crispies. I have a quick look round for Lemmy but apart from a small pile of biscuit crumbs by the washing machine there is no sign of him.

I switch on the TV and Dana Devene is on

already. You can tell she is professional because she has high heels on very early in the morning, when normal people are mostly hopping around looking for their other slipper. She is walking up a darkish street with a microphone in one hand and a huge bunch of flowers in the other. I cannot believe she will be doing this outside our house in a couple of days. I eat my Coco-Crispies quickly to stop me feeling faint.

Dana rings the bell of a house and a woman in a flowery dress answers the door. Dana shrieks, "Surprise!" and stuffs the flowers right in the woman's face and I let out a bit of a groan because if she does that to my mum, my mum will probably do something really unladylike back. I am no longer full up of relieved, I am full up of worried again.

The lady is called Janine, which is a good name for a mother, a bit normal and a bit interesting. My mum is called Amanda, which is very boring because it is like loads of other people's mums. I wonder if I can persuade her to change it by Thursday.

Dana and "Keep-Up Jim", the cameraman (I call him that because that's what Dana always says to him), force their way past Janine and into her living room.

Then Dana starts shrieking, "This is so geeeeorgeous!"

Janine's house is totally full up with frilly things. She has curtains with special tassely bits to tie them back. There are lacy bits on the lampshades and tablecloths everywhere. There are crocheted blankets thrown over all the chairs and so many cushions on the sofa that everyone has to stand up.

"Wow!" says Dana, stroking the curtains and cushions covers like they are fluffy kittens. "What a beautiful home!"

Janine, who is still picking petals out of her hair, squeaks, "Thank you."

And I am thinking actually it is not very beautiful. There is so much fabric everywhere, it must be like living inside someone's wardrobe. (Not mine, obviously – one with stuff in it.)

"And this chest of drawers is so shabby . . . so shabby chic!" says Dana.

"I scratched it myself," Janine says proudly. "I love to sew and craft to create the perfect home for my family. I also sell my designs and give the money to a home for unloved donkeys."

She wipes a little tear from her eye, and Dana looks a bit sad for about half a second then she says brightly, "And that dress looks . . . home-made."

"Yes, I made it myself, from a vintage pattern," Janine says, cheering up.

"Thought so," says Dana. "It's very . . . retro."

"I also make all the children's clothes," Janine says, pointing to a whole pile of little kids who are sitting in the corner wearing old-fashioned-looking clothes. Dana picks on a very cute little girl with ginger plaits and a patchwork dress. "Hello," she coos, bending down towards her, "what's your name?"

"Melitha," she says and smiles to show her front teeth are missing, which seems to make her even more cute.

"And maybe your mum is a Mum in a Million, Melissa?" Dana says, and I think it proves how professional she is that she doesn't mess that line up.

"Yeth, she'th the bethtetht in the world," Melissa says.

"Try not to spit, dear," mutters Dana, rubbing her cheek and standing up quickly.

"And what is this, Janine?" asks Dana, picking up a throw from the back of the sofa with two fingers.

"That's a memory quilt," Janine explains. "I made it from scraps of the children's old clothes and baby blankets, oh and my granny's apron after she died."

Dana drops the quilt hastily and wipes her hand on her skirt. "Well, this is all totally delightful, Janine. It's been fabulous to meet you and good luck with being our Mum in a Million!"

Everyone smiles at the camera and they switch back to the studio. I switch off.

A one-legged giraffe is just not going to cut it. I wonder if we could quickly knock up a memory quilt by Thursday, but I think all our memories got sent to the charity shop ages ago.

At least Janine doesn't seem to make cakes. She probably couldn't fight her way through all the fabric to get to the kitchen. I think we will just have to do really well in the baking, which is very easy to think but a lot harder to do.

While I am thinking about this, Uncle Clive comes downstairs. He says he is up early to try to catch Lemmy before Mum and Dad come down

and ask him why he is crawling round the kitchen floor with a piece of cheese and a shoebox.

"The early bird catches the worm, Emily," he says, from under the kitchen table, and I am a bit worried that he has lost another pet for a minute but then I realise he is just using a metaphor, which is what Mrs Lovetofts is always trying to get us to do, and I think I'll remember it in case it's useful for a merit mark.

I decide to go and get dressed. I tiptoe into the bedroom so as not to wake Clover up, but the strange thing about tiptoeing is that it makes all the floorboards squeak much louder. Clover opens her eyes, looks at me through the bars of the cot and smiles.

"Morning, Clover," I say. "I am not saying *good* morning because it is not good. I have to turn Mum into a super baker and I don't know what to do."

"Kai," says Clover, which is another new word.

"I don't know how to make cakes properly. Last time I tried it was a total disaster—"

"Kai, kai," Clover says.

"—although that was mostly because Chloe was there."

"KAI!" Clover shouts.

I look at her and she is staring right back and then I smile. "That is a brilliant idea! Why didn't you say so earlier?"

Even though Uncle Clive is an early bird he has not caught any worms, or rats. When I get back downstairs he is sitting in the living room looking fed up.

"I don't think Lemmy wants to come back," he

says. "I think he is enjoying his freedom. Which is exactly what Daisy said." He sighs heavily. "What am I doing wrong, Emily?"

I think this is one of those questions it's better not to answer because I could give him a list, starting with his feet, followed by his jacket, his hair and his motorbike smell, but I don't think he really wants to hear it. Poor Uncle Clive, or Uncle *Kai* as Clover calls him.

"Cheer up," I say, "you make the best brownies, all my friends loved them. I'm glad you're here," which at the moment is totally not a lie because I need him for my plan.

He gives me a big smile, and I realise this is the first time I have seen him smile properly for ages. He looks quite nice when he smiles, well, apart from his chipped front tooth.

"Thanks, Emily," he says, ruffling my hair so

much I will have to spend an hour combing it out later. "I like being here with you and Flora, too."

"Clover," I say.

"Sorry."

"I'll bet you couldn't teach Mum how to make cakes, though."

"Oh, it's a bet, is it?" laughs Uncle Clive. "Well, your mum is a very talented lady, I'll bet I could teach her."

"If you do I'll . . . I'll polish your boots for you."

"You're on!" Uncle Clive says. "Those boots haven't been cleaned for years."

I feel a bit faint at the thought and have to quickly remind myself that it's better than being arrested.

"Can we do it tonight?" I ask.

"Fine with me. Not sure your mum will have time, though. She's very busy with her shed project," he says with a wink.

CHAPTER FIFTEEN

Hearts and Cauliflowers

Still Tuesday

I meet Zuzanna to go to school and she is already talking about Janine before I have even finished mumbling, "Sorry, I'm late" (three minutes, front door got stuck).

In fact, she is so excited she has even forgotten to frown.

"Wasn't her house lovely?"

183

she says, "all those home-made things and vintage too. That's what you need in your house, Emily. Have you taught your mum to sew yet?"

"Err . . . kind of," I say.

"Shabby chic is totally the way to go," she says. "Mostly it's chipping the paint off furniture and hanging up wicker hearts."

"Wicker what?"

Zuzanna scrabbles in her bag and hands me a couple of heart-shaped straw decorations. "Stick a couple of these around," she says. "My mum won't miss them, she has loads."

"Thanks," I say, although they look a bit scruffy to me.

"Here, give me the plan," Zuzanna says.

I pull the crumpled piece of paper out of my bag. Zuzanna stops, leans up against a wall and writes:

on the bottom. "And," she continues, "you maybe want to look a bit more cute. I mean, Melissa was soooo sweet."

"I guess so," I say, trying to imagine what I'd look like in pigtails and patchwork. "Although maybe I'll just get Clover to do the cute bit."

"You know you need to be getting on with this, Emily. You've only got a couple of days."

"There's quite a lot to do," I say.

"Luckily, Chloe and I are here to support you," Zuzanna says. "Although, personally I would never have entered my mother for a competition like this. Especially if I had yours," she says pushing open the school door.

At school it is total Harvest Festival madness. We have to line cardboard boxes with straw and fill them with harvest stuff for all the old people. I suppose the food is a good thing. I'm not sure what they are supposed to do with all the straw, though. Zuzanna says it's good for keeping you warm and they could stuff it in their socks but that sounds a bit itchy to me.

Mrs Lovetofts is a bit stressed because she has "courgettes coming out of her ears" and not enough nice things to go in the boxes.

"Vegetables are all very well," she says, "but you can't dunk a carrot in your tea."

Which actually you could, especially if you were a very healthy sort of old person, but I don't argue because I don't think she's in the mood.

Mrs Lovetofts says we can decorate our cardboard boxes first if we like. Gross-Out Gavin and Alfie Balfour have done pictures of guns and tanks and soldiers all over theirs. Gross-Out says it is to remind the old people of the war, but Mrs Lovetofts says it is "inappropriate" and makes them cover it up with some pages ripped out of *Gardeners' World*.

Nicole and Babette have done Nike ticks all over theirs and written "Just Do It" on the side, to encourage the old people to do more exercise.

I suggest we could decorate our box with glitter and stuff to get the old people excited about Christmas. "Which is exactly fifty days away," I say. But Zuzanna says it's not good for old people to get too excited, so she and Chloe write "Happy Harvest" all over the box in bubble writing and I am not in the mood to argue as I have thought of a new problem.

It is a very good idea of Clover's to get Uncle Clive to help Mum make a cake, but how am I going to persuade Mum to do it?

I can't just say, "Basically, Mum, can you go and bake a cake with Uncle Clive?", because she will just say, "Basically, no."

I am thinking about this all day and not getting any further than "Ummmm" when Mrs Lovetofts finally comes to the rescue.

"Just before you go home, everyone," she says at the end of the day, "we really do need some more yummy things to put in our Harvest Boxes. I know they are meant to celebrate Harvest but there's only so much cauliflower an old person can take. Here's a letter for your parents."

*Dear parents, carers and those fulfilling a
similar function,
    The children will be having
a Harvest Festival in the
hall on Thursday. We*

are putting together food parcels to be
distributed to elderly local residents. If you
have any contributions they would be most
welcome. Especially cakes and biscuits and
other special treats. Please note we have enough
marrows and courgettes already.

Thank you for your support,
Mrs Lovetofts
Harvest Festival Co-ordinator

Now that's very nearly homework. Mum will
have to buckle down to some baking!

CHAPTER SIXTEEN

What's in a Cake?

Still Tuesday

When I get home from school the kitchen is still clean! And even the living room looks OK-ish now that the pipes have gone, although you do get the feeling that something's missing, they were sort of becoming part of the family. I'm not actually sure where Mum is though. I walked home with Zuzanna, who was still going on about

Janine's house, and got in to find Uncle Clive snoring on the sofa, Clover snoring in her baby chair and Lemmy eating a cream cracker in the corner but no Mum anywhere. I made a sort of half-hearted grab for Lemmy but he did a little leap and shot off back to the kitchen and I just know he was smiling.

Uncle Clive can't make cakes if he is snoring and Mum can't make cakes if she is not here, so I have two things to sort out before I have even got my coat off. My life is much too full of responsibilities. I put the TV on loudly. Uncle Clive wakes up with a bit of a grunt.

"Do you know where Mum is?" I ask.

"Oh, err . . . must have dropped off for a second," he says, pushing his hair out of his face. "She's down in her shed. I'm looking after Flora."

"Clover."

"Sorry."

I hear the back door shut. "Hello, love," Mum says as I go into the kitchen. She is washing paint brushes in the sink.

I try not to get stressed about the sink getting messy.

"What have you got there?" she says.

"Harvest Festival letter. We need to make a cake."

"A cake? Why? I normally give them some courgettes," she says, looking confused.

"No more courgettes, they've got too many."

"So have we," Mum mutters. "How about a marrow?"

"Mum. It says cake."

"You know baking's not really my thing, Emily."

"Uncle Clive says he'll help, he's really good."

"Good idea," Mum says. "You and Uncle Clive can do it together," and she dries her hands and starts to leave the kitchen.

"Noooo," I say, trying to think faster than my brain wants to. "I can't . . . err. Loads of homework. Tons. Mrs Lovetofts has gone homework mad. No time to bake."

"Well, Uncle Clive can do it on his own then," Mum says.

"But . . . he'll just make a massive mess – Gran will be cross if it's all messy in here after she cleaned it, won't she?"

Mum lets out a big sigh. "Oh I suppose so," she says. Then she smiles. "Actually this might be quite a good idea. Ask Uncle Clive to come in here then. Now where did I see that recipe?"

I am banned from the kitchen and have to look after Clover. I should be pleased that Mum is finally making cakes but I'm not so sure now. When Mum does that funny smile you can bet that something is up.

I think I might make a quick start on getting our living room to look more shabby chic so I prop up Mum's one-legged giraffe on the mantelpiece, in between the clay candle-holder I made in Year Three and Chloe's hammock postcard. I think the hammock postcard looks a bit unshabby so I give it to Clover to chew a bit and then it looks much better.

We don't have any crocheted throws but there is an old pink towel on the clothes airer so I hang that over the back of the chair and plump up the two cushions that, to be fair, do look very vintage already. (We only have two cushions because the rest have been thrown out for smelling of baby sick.) I hang Zuzanna's wicker hearts on either side of the TV and take a step back.

"What do you think?" I ask Clover.

"Bleh," she says.

Which I think translates as, "You'd better hope the baking's good."

Actually, the baking sounds like it's going quite well. There is a lot of clattering and banging in the kitchen and a loud whirring noise which sounds like the food processor on overdrive, but soon there is also a very delicious smell.

I need a bit of a distraction so I am glad it is time to message Bella.

 Emily says: Bella? Hi.

 Bella says: Hi. What's up?

 Emily says: Mum is in the kitchen - baking a cake!!!!!!!

 Bella says: Hey, that's great. How did you get her to do that?

 Emily says: Long story. I've even got her to do some sewing but there's no way I'm going to get her into a dress.

 Bella says: I saw her in a dress once.

196

Emily says: When?

 Bella says: When we had a sleepover.

 Emily says: That was a Marks & Spencer nightshirt.

 Bella says: Well, it might look all right . . . with a belt.

 Emily says: Hang on. BRB. Mum just called to say cake is done!

Sitting in the middle of the kitchen table is a cake. It is round and has some creamy stuff in the middle. It looks like . . . a cake.

"What do you think?" asks Mum.

The cake looks good and

197

it smells good. I'm not sure what to say except, "I think . . . I think . . . it's good, I think."

Mum smiles. "I think it's pretty good too," she says.

I sniff at it cautiously. "What's in the middle?"

"Buttercream."

I examine the cake very closely. It really does look very nice.

"Here," Mum says. "We made a small one for the family. Try a bit."

I take a bite of cake. It's sweet and moist and crumbly. It's fine! In fact, it's lovely. Dana Devene will be bowled over. My mum can totally bake.

"It's great," I say.

"Don't know why your mum doesn't make cakes more often," Uncle Clive says. "She's very creative."

"Creative?" I say and I take another big bite.

"Yes," Uncle Clive says. "Who would have thought of courgette cake! Great idea."

"Phwaurrgette cake!" I splutter and drop the slice of cake on to the table. "Ewwwwwww!"

"You just said it was great." Mum laughs.

"Courgette cake!" I say again. I don't seem to be able to say anything else.

Uncle Clive laughs too. "You like carrot cake, Emily. Why not courgette?"

"But courgettes aren't meant to go in cake – they are meant to go in, in . . ." Actually I don't know what they are meant to go in. Mostly I think it would be best if they went in the bin.

"I'm sure your teacher will love it," Mum says. "Now sorry but I've got to get on with my shed," and she goes off leaving me with Uncle Clive and the courgette cake.

"Don't worry, Emily," Uncle Clive says. "You can make cake out of lots of things: beetroot, bananas. It's all very chilled out in the baking world."

Uncle Clive puts the school cake into a cake tin and presses the lid down firmly. "Lemmy-proof," he says with a wink. And I think, *Don't worry, Lemmy probably has better taste.*

Emily says: I'm back.

 Bella says: How was the cake?

 Emily says: Interesting.

 Bella says: Interesting as in "Delicious" or interesting as in "Mary Berry just fainted"?

 Emily says: Interesting as in COURGETTE CAKE!!!!!

 Bella says: Noooooo!

 Emily says: It looks OK. As long as Dana doesn't ask what it's made of it might be OK. I still have to get her into a dress though. She does have a dress she used to wear for work. But how am I going to get her to wear it on Thursday?

Bella says: Hide her jeans?

I am just thinking this might be a good idea but I'm not sure where to hide ten pairs of jeans, when Lemmy scoots across the top of the computer screen.

 Emily says: One more thing.

 Bella says: Yes.

 Emily says: You don't know how to catch rats, do you?

CHAPTER SEVENTEEN

Perfect Penny

Wednesday

Next morning it is someone else's turn to be embarrassed by Dana, live on camera. I am the only one awake to see it because Clover decided to stay awake all night and Mum had to take her into her bedroom so I could sleep. Sometimes it is like our house runs on Australian time.

This time Dana is creeping up the drive of a very big house.

"Oooh, this is posh, isn't it?" she whispers to the camera. She rings the bell and it goes "bong" and for a minute I think it will be answered by a butler who won't at all appreciate being thumped in the face by a bunch of flowers. However, the door is opened by a woman wearing a cream blouse with pearls round her neck.

"Surprise!" says Dana and tries to stuff the bouquet at the lady, but ends up stumbling into the hall when the lady takes a step to the side. A large brown dog starts barking loudly.

"Do be quiet, Hunter," says the lady. "I'm sorry," she continues, "Hunter doesn't like strangers." Hunter growls menacingly.

Dana mutters, "Nice doggie," and backs away. Then she pulls herself together and does her big toothy smile for the camera. "Hello, Penny.

We hear that you are a Mum in a Million!" She holds out the flowers.

"How very nice," says Penny, looking at the flowers as if they are a bit mouldy. "Put them over there, would you," she adds, pointing to a side table. "I'll deal with them later."

Dana says, "Could we take a look at your lovely home?"

Penny leads the way into a huge living room.

"Keep up, Jim," Dana says, hurrying after her.

The room has leather sofas, paintings that look like they come from an art gallery and dark wood tables with large bowls of white flowers.

Dana looks around. "It's very tidy, isn't it?"

"It's tasteful, Dana," says Penny.

"That's it exactly," beams Dana. "Tasteful."

I look around our living room, which is utterly cluttery, filled with washing and plastic baby toys. I don't think it's tasteful. I stuff a couple of rattles behind a cushion.

"So tell us, Penny, why are you a Mum in a Million?" Dana says.

Penny gives a little laugh. "Oh, I really couldn't say," she says.

"Oh, right then, let's move on to the—"

"Unless of course it's because of all the work I do for charity, and I run my own *tasteful* flower-arranging courses and I cook a three-course meal for my children every evening and of course I'm a school governor—"

"Goodness! I understand you are also an excellent baker, Penny," Dana says.

"I dabble." Penny smiles. "The children like it." Hunter growls. "Oh, and Hunter too, of course, he'll eat anything."

"I can well believe it," Dana mutters and skirts past him into the kitchen.

Two bored-looking children are sitting by a table eating breakfast, with proper cups and bowls and jugs of juice and even folded napkins. The only time we ever all have breakfast at the table is when someone comes to stay and Mum is showing off. Mostly it's shovel down the cornflakes while trying to get your shoes on. And I am very surprised to see Penny's children have their school uniform on already and the girl even has her hair braided. I suppose that's the downside of having a perfect home – you have to look the part, or you're out.

"These are Clementina and Milo, my little angels," says Penny.

"So," says Dana, "do you think your mum is a Mum in a Million?"

The children look at each other.

"Speak up, Clementina," Penny says. "Ms Devene can't hear you."

"S'pose so," Clementina says and yawns.

"That's lovely," Dana says. "Why do you think she's so great?"

Milo looks at his mum. "I forgot," he says. "What was it again?"

"It's because I help you with your homework, play lots of fun games and bake really lovely cakes, isn't it?" Penny snaps.

"Oh, yeah, that's it," Milo says, and takes a bite of toast.

"So, which one of you nominated your mum as a Mum in a Million?" Dana says.

"I did," says Clementina.

"And why is that?"

"Because she told me to."

Penny laughs a bit too loudly. "Of course I didn't, darling," she says. "Children are funny, aren't they?" She takes Dana by the arm. "The cakes are over here."

"Keep up, Jim," Dana says.

The camera pans over to a display of cakes at the back of the kitchen. I nearly choke on my Coco-Crispies. There are cupcakes with multi-coloured frosting and shimmering sparkles, little sponge cakes with cream and strawberries and pastel-coloured iced buns. And right in the middle is a towering three-tiered cake dripping with white and brown chocolate and covered in pink sugar roses.

Dana gasps. "These are fantastic, Penny. Can I try one?" She reaches out her hand and Hunter growls. "On second thoughts," says Dana, snatching her hand back, "mustn't forget the diet. So from super baker Penny and her two err ... delightful children – back to the studio!"

At school Chloe and Zuzanna have lots to say about Penny.

"Wasn't her home fabulous?" Zuzanna says. "So elegant and simple."

"Yes and so ... big," Chloe says. "Almost as big as mine."

"Well, I can't make my house any bigger, can I?" I say.

"Maybe you could try to make it more tasteful," Chloe says. "You know, artworks and flower arrangements. No clutter."

"You might want to smarten yourself up a bit too," Zuzanna says. "Definitely no summer dresses, and see if you can iron your shirt."

"And you totally need to learn how to smize," Chloe says.

"Smize?"

"Yes, it's eye smiling. All the celebs do it." She pulls a face that looks a lot like that python from *The Jungle Book.*

"I think what Chloe means is, try to look smart, tasteful, cheerful but intelligent," Zuzanna says.

"I thought you said I should be cute, retro and shabby chic," I say.

"Oh, Emily," Chloe says, "shabby chic is so yesterday."

CHAPTER EIGHTEEN

{ Dress to Impress }

Still Wednesday

I get home to find Mum and Clover are being Australian again and are fast asleep upstairs but I don't mind because I think it is a good chance to get our living room to look a bit more tasteful. In fact, I have decided to go for both tasteful and shabby chic mixed together so that Dana can take her pick.

I bought my mum a tasteful art picture from

the School Table Top Sale (or the School "Dump Your Rubbish on Someone Else" Sale as my dad calls it). It's a painting of some people dancing on a beach with some other people holding umbrellas. I think it's very nice. Mum keeps saying she'll put it up one day but it has been in the cupboard under the stairs for ages. I drag it out and give it a rub with my sleeve to get the dust off. Then I think I will have to bang a nail into the wall so I can put it up. I go down to the shed to find a hammer but the shed is locked and there is a sign on the door: "Mum's Project. Keep Out. This means you, Emily." I am getting very worried about what she is doing in there. I mean I hope she's not building a space rocket or making a time machine or something. Those sort of things always go wrong if you do them in a shed. Just ask Wallace and Gromit.

I decide I will just have to balance the picture on top of the high bookshelves and hope for the best. I climb up on a chair and it balances just right. Then I need to make a tasteful flower arrangement. This is not easy as I don't have any flowers. Luckily, I get a bit of Emily Sparkes creativityness and remember the Ikebana flower and twig stuff that Dana Devene did on TV. And also luckily there are still a few dandelions in the lawn, so I put one in a mug with a couple of twigs from the garden and stick it next to the TV. I'm not sure if it's tasteful or shabby chic, but Dana can decide that.

I have just finished when Mum comes downstairs. She is wearing some old leggings and Dad's sweatshirt, which might actually be vintage, but not in a good way.

"Guess what, Emily?" she says when she has made herself a cup of coffee, eaten an apple and moaned about how tired she is for five minutes. "I'm coming into your school tomorrow to do a little talk at the Harvest Festival."

How come my mum always manages to make another problem just as I am sorting out the current disaster?

"A talk?" I squeak. "What about?"

"Vegetables," she says, as if this is something that normal people do.

"But, who? Why? What?" I sound like Mrs Lovetofts when she tries to get us to write better stories. I can't seem to get a proper sentence out.

"Mr Meakin has asked me to give a little talk on the importance of growing food and eating healthily. Isn't that great? Dad's taking the morning off to look after Clover. I'm quite excited."

"Great," I say, already trying to work

out if there's any way of hiding when you are sitting in the middle of the assembly hall with two hundred other children staring at you, while they try to imagine what it would be like to have such an embarrassing parent. "Thanks, Mum. Any time you want to stop with the character-building experiences would be fine with me, though."

"Hmmm?" Mum says. She doesn't seem to be listening. She's pushing an apple pip around the worktop with her finger.

I go upstairs to update the plan. On the way past I try to peep into my room but the door is shut tight again and I can hear Uncle Clive whistling.

In Clover's room I pull out the crumpled sheet of paper.

The Plan ~ 2 3 4

By Chloe, Zuzanna and Emily

★ Make a plan ✓
★ Tidy up house ✓
★ Vote for the NV Boyz on X factor ✓
★ ~~Someone~~ Emily teach Emily's mum
to sew something ✓
★ ~~Someone~~ Uncle Clive teach
Emily's mum to bake a cake ✓
★ Someone sort out Emily's
mum's clothes and hair
★ Make your House
Shabby Chic ✓
★ Make your House Tasteful ✓

(added by Chloe this afternoon)

I have just finished when there is a tap on the door, and it is Uncle Clive.

"Ah, Emily!" he says, waving an enormous shoe

brush at me. "I think I won our little bet." He gives me his big chipped-tooth grin and dumps his huge boots in the doorway.

I am getting utterly exhausted by this whole week. I don't even care about going to London because there is no way we are going to win and, even if we did, shopping with Chloe and trudging round a museum with Zuzanna doesn't sound like much fun. If it wasn't for trying to keep out of prison I would just about give up.

After about an hour of polishing I have managed to get Uncle Clive's boots to look as if they might belong in the human world, although they have splashes of what seems like purple paint all over them which I definitely can't get off. Then I have to get back to the last bit of the plan.

My mum totally needs to wear something nice by exactly tomorrow morning. I need some creativityness but the boot polishing has used up all my energy. I don't know what to do. Janine had a vintage-type dress and Penny had a blouse and pearls, and now half the country is going to see my mum in a gardening jumper.

I have a big lie-down on the camp bed. Bella's suggestion of hiding all Mum's jeans was quite good, but I have given up on it after looking in Mum's wardrobe. She has loads of pairs and, as I have found out with the Allotment Club poster, there is no such thing as a Mum-proof hiding place anyway.

I am trying to concentrate but I keep worrying about her talk at Harvest Festival. I need to prioritise. Harvest Festival is just going to be humiliation in front of the whole school – Dana Devene is going to humiliate me in front of the whole world if I don't get my mum into something tidy soon.

Honestly, I don't even know why Mum is doing this Harvest Festival thing. I think she's got a bit of a thing about Mr Meakin; she goes along with all his suggestions. And then I have a little tiny bit of an idea that just might work.

"Mum," I say, walking into the kitchen where it looks like yet another pasta bake is under way.

"Yes, love," Mum says.

"Can I use the iron to iron my school skirt?"

Mum looks very surprised. "Are you feeling all right?" she says.

"Yes, it's just that it's Harvest Festival tomorrow and everyone is expected to look smart."

"Really?" Mum says.

"Oh yes, even the teachers wear their best clothes. You know, *dresses* and things."

"Dresses?"

 "Yes, well, not the men teachers obviously, they just wear suits and ties, sometimes bow ties ... top hats, that sort of thing."

"Top hats!"

"Mr Meakin always looks very smart. He says it's

essential to dress well on important occasions . . .
What are you wearing?"

"Well, I don't know, I mean, I hadn't really
thought about it. Perhaps I'd better go and have a
look," she says, drying her hands.

"Good idea, I'll come with you."

Actually, once she starts looking, Mum has
loads of nice clothes, she just never wears them.

"I'm not sure if any of these things still fit me,"
she says. "I have just had a baby, you know."

"That was weeks ago," I say. "Try this one on."

Mum tries on a blue dress with a flared skirt. She
looks very nice, although not at all like
my mum.

"See, that fits fine. Now all you need
to do is your hair."

"My hair?"

"Well, you can't really wear Granddad's flat cap
with that, can you?"

Mum sighs. "I suppose not," she says, rummaging

in the cupboard for the hair straighteners. "This is all getting very complicated."

"Mr Meakin will be very impressed," I say, slipping out of the room.

I get my schoolbag and pull out the plan

<u>The Plan - ~~2~~ ~~3~~ ~~4~~ 5</u>
By Chloe, Zuzanna and Emily

★ Make a plan ✓
★ Tidy up house ✓
★ Vote for the NV Boyz on X factor ✓
★ ~~Someone~~ Emily teach Emily's mum to sew ✓
★ ~~Someone~~ Uncle Clive teach Emily's mum to bake a cake ✓
★ ~~Someone~~ Emily sort out Emily's mum's clothes and hair ✓
★ Make your House Shabby Chic ✓
★ Make your House Tasteful ✓

That's it! I've done it. I have made my mum perfect in four days. Well, OK, not exactly perfect. My mum might not be able to sew like Janine or bake like Penny but at least they can't arrest me for competition fraud. Mum is going to look normal, and we have a tasteful painting in the living room and even the courgette cake looks OK from a distance. Dana always asks the kids what they think so I just need to keep her talking for long enough so that she doesn't look at anything too closely. Yes, I am ready for tomorrow. Bring on Dana Devene.

CHAPTER NINETEEN

Surprise, Surprise (Again)!

Thursday

I have hardly slept all night. I keep thinking I hear the doorbell ringing or somebody clip-clopping up the path in very high heels. I got up before it was even light and put my school uniform on. I have got a flowery headband on as well, just in case Dana prefers cute kids to sensible ones. I creep downstairs and turn on the living room light to see— more copper pipes! I can't believe it. Dad has obviously decided his new ones are not safe in the garage. He has put them back, right in the middle of the living room. They are utterly ruining the effect of my interior-decorating efforts. They don't look even a tiny bit shabby chic or tasteful. I balance a wicker heart on top and hope it helps them blend in. There's no time to do anything else now.

I set the table in the kitchen with bowls and cups. We don't have any cloth napkins but I dot a few pieces of kitchen roll about and that will have to do. I feel too sick to eat anything anyway.

Luckily, Clover went back to Greenwich Mean Time last night so Mum is already getting up too. She wanders into the kitchen to make tea wearing her dressing gown with the ripped pocket. "Goodness, Emily, what's all this stuff on the table?" she asks.

"I thought it would be nice if we had breakfast properly today," I say. "You know, like they do on orange juice adverts."

"No one in an orange juice advert ever has a two-month-old baby." Mum yawns and pours her tea.

"Don't you think you'd better get dressed for the Harvest Festival, Mum?" I say. "We don't want to be late."

"I'm sure I've got time for a cup of tea," Mum says. I glance at the clock. Dana will be having her last-minute lip gloss applied by now.

"You can take your tea with you. Really, Mr Meakin is very into punctuality, it's one of his favourite things, that and shiny black shoes," I say, giving her a firm push in the direction of the stairs.

Mum grumbles and mumbles but thankfully heads off upstairs. I have just finished plumping up the two cushions and adjusting the pink towel when there is a knock on the door. I can't believe it. She can't be here already.

"Mum!" I shout. "There's someone at the door!"

"Well, answer it then, Emily," she calls back downstairs.

"I err . . . I think you should."

"For goodness' sake, Emily, it's probably the postman. I'm not dressed yet."

There is another tap on the door. I definitely don't want my mum on national TV in her underwear. I will have to handle it myself, as usual.

I run to the front door and hurl Uncle Clive's shiny boots to one side. I stand with my back to the wall to avoid getting punched in the face with a bouquet of flowers and yank open the door.

"Welcome to our lovely home!" I say.

"Thanks," Chloe says, "although I think 'lovely' is a bit over the top."

"Chloe! What are you doing here?" I hiss.

"We thought we'd support you, of course. I mean, what are friends for?" Chloe says.

"We?"

"Hi," Zuzanna says, stepping out from behind Chloe.

"You'd better come in," I say, looking up and down the street for any sign of Dana. Fortunately there's nothing yet.

Chloe and Zuzanna go into the living room. Zuzanna looks around. "Is this supposed to be shabby chic or tasteful?" she says.

"It's a combination," I say.

"And I'm still not convinced by your modern art sculpture," Chloe says, poking the pipes with her foot.

"Come on, Emily, turn the TV on," Zuzanna says. "We don't want to miss it."

"We can't miss it, can we?" I say. "It's going to be here." I press the remote and the TV clicks on.

"And now it's time to go over to Dana Devene, who's somewhere about to surprise another mum," says the TV presenter in the studio. "Dana, can you hear me?"

The screen flicks to Dana Devene, standing in

her high heels and very shiny lipstick, at the end of our road. I feel faint.

"It's her!" Chloe says. "OM actual G! Smize everyone, smize." She scrabbles in her bag and pulls out a notebook.

"What's that for?" Zuzanna says.

"It's my autograph book," Chloe says.

Zuzanna takes it off her and flicks through it. "But it's totally empty," she says. "What happened to Jessie J and Olly?"

"It's new, my other one was too full up," Chloe says snatching it back.

"Will you two shush!" I say.

It is a very strange feeling to watch a celebrity creeping up your street on the TV. It is an even stranger feeling when you notice that creeping up a little way behind her is someone else.

"Like, who is that old bag lady woman person behind her?" Chloe asks.

"It could be a celebrity stalker," Zuzanna says.

Dana clip-clops closer, bouquet in hand. She passes Mr Bevan-at-number-thirty-seven's and I see his curtains twitch.

Now she is walking up our path. I can hardly breathe.

"Here I am, outside this ... very ordinary-looking house, about to surprise another Mum in a Million!" she says in a loud whisper.

"Not so fast, young lady!" The old woman grabs hold of Dana Devene by the elbow.

Gran!

"Neighbourhood Watch," Gran says. "There've been some thefts in this area."

"Gran! No!" I shout at the TV.

"We can't have people creeping about willy-nilly," Gran says. "Can I see your ID?"

"I can assure you I have never done anything willy-nilly," says Dana, trying to wriggle her arm free.

I dash to the front door and yank it open. "Gran! What are you doing?"

"Don't worry, love. I've got it covered," Gran says. "Can someone call for back-up?"

"Back-up? Gran, it's Dana Devene," I say. "Off the telly!"

"I don't care who she is," Gran says, then she pauses. "Off the telly? Oooh, do you know Carole the weather girl?"

"What on earth is going on?" says Mum's voice from over my shoulder.

Dana wriggles her elbow out from Gran's grip and mutters "Mad old bat" in a very not celebrity way, before putting on her big smile again.

"Congratulations!" she says to Mum. "You have been nominated for Mum in a Million!" She shoves the flowers forward and I duck out of the way just in time to avoid a bouquet bashing.

Mum takes the flowers and looks very confused. "I think you'd better come in," she says.

"Good idea," Gran says. "There's some funny people around here. Any tea on the go?"

Mum, Gran, Dana, Keep-Up Jim, Chloe, Zuzanna and I all squash back into the living room. There are also two random ladies who must have something to do with the TV. Everyone is talking at once and trying not to trip over the copper pipes. Mum is attempting to get people to sit down and Gran is asking how everyone likes their tea and I can't believe that Mum is wearing her old gardening clothes after all, including the flat cap. I am just wondering if we can get away with calling a holey jumper shabby chic when she turns to Dana and says, "Can you please tell me what is going on?"

"Your daughter, Emily, has nominated you as a Mum in a Million," Dana says.

"She has?"

"Yes, so we've come to have a look around your ... err ... stylish home and find out about your love of sewing and baking."

"My what? Emily, what is all this—?" Mum begins but she is interrupted by Dad who comes down the stairs in his pyjama bottoms carrying Clover.

"Oh! What a cute baby," Dana says. "Jim, get a good shot of the kid," she mutters.

"I think she's done a poo," Dad says and hands Clover to Mum.

"How charming," Dana says, backing away.

Mum swiftly hands Clover back to Dad. "You said you'd look after her this morning."

Dad sighs. "I didn't really mean nappies," he grumbles, and heads for the stairs with Clover. He looks back over his shoulder. "Bit early for a coffee morning, isn't it?"

"Daa," Clover says. Which means, *Told you he's not very observant.*

"So," Dana says, looking around uncertainly, "what style would you say you have decorated your living room in?"

"It's a cross between shabby chic and tasteful, isn't it, Mum?" I say quickly.

"Yes, I see, *shabby taste* maybe," says Dana. "And what statement are you trying to make with the display of copper pipes?"

"It's a modern art installation," Chloe says, smizing in Dana's direction. "We're getting one put in next week. You'd be very welcome to come round and see. We also have two swimming pools, a home cine—"

"Not now, Chloe," Zuzanna says, nudging her with her elbow.

"And I see you have some more traditional art here," Dana says, pointing to the picture balanced on the bookshelves above her head. "Err . . . is it me or is it moving?"

I look up to where she is pointing. The picture is definitely wobbling, and from where I am standing

I can just see a long tail hanging out from behind it.

"Oh dear," Dana says, trying to back away but getting hemmed in by the pipes, "I think it's going to fall!"

"Lemmy!" a voice shouts from the doorway. Uncle Clive appears and makes a dash for the bookshelves. "I'm going to catch him!" he yells, but his huge feet get tangled up with the copper pipes and he crashes down right in front of Dana Devene, knocking her sideways against the wall. The picture wobbles one last time and also crashes down, on Uncle Clive's head.

"Oh my stars!" Dana Devene says. "I could have been killed. This place is a death trap. Except, of course," she says, putting on her glossy smile again, "for this big brave man." She kneels down next to Uncle Clive. "Are you all right? Someone get this super hunky man a cup of coffee."

A few minutes later Uncle Clive is sitting on the

sofa with a pack of frozen peas on his head and a cup of coffee in his hand. Dana is sitting next to him talking to the camera. "I think this just proves that the old-fashioned English gentleman is still alive and well, if slightly bruised," she says with a smile. "I hope you all saw how this brave man jumped across the room shouting, 'Let me. I'm going to catch it,' and saved me from a serious blow to the head. What a hero." Dana gives Uncle Clive a kiss on the cheek, leaving a glossy lipstick mark, and he gives her a chipped-tooth grin back.

"I'm sorry to interrupt," Mum says, "but I really need to be going soon."

Dana pats her hair. "Yes, of course, back to you." She stands up and turns to the camera. "Now, after all that excitement, back to our *special* mum." Then 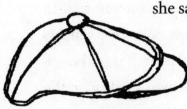 she says to my mum, "Can you tell us about the clothes you're wearing today? That hat is especially . . . unusual?"

Mum looks at me a little guiltily. "I'm doing a talk at the Harvest Festival today. I was going to wear a dress but I thought as the talk is about growing and gardening I'd—"

"Dress up as a scarecrow? Well, I'm sure the children will appreciate it." Dana laughs. "Now, can we see some of your sewing and baking?"

"Baking?" Mum says. "Yes, I do a bit of baking. Come through to the kitchen."

Dana follows her through and I am thinking, *Thank goodness she made that cake*, and also, *I really hope she doesn't say what's in it*. In fact, I am thinking so much that I don't notice what she's about to do until it's too late.

Mum opens the fridge and takes out a dish. "Pasta bake," she says. "I make it all the time. This is left over from last night. It's very economical."

Dana peers into the dish like she thinks something might actually crawl out of it (although this is not likely as I think Lemmy is still behind the

236

bookshelves). "Leftover pasta bake . . . err, right. And what are those slightly slimy green things?" She points a glossy fingernail.

"Courgettes. From the garden," Mum says proudly.

"Well, of course, there is all sorts of baking, and this is definitely all sorts," Dana says, looking a bit queasy.

I can't keep quiet any longer. "But, Mum, what about the cake you baked for the Harvest Festival!"

"Oh yes," Mum says. "I forgot about that. Cake isn't proper food, is it?"

I grab the cake tin from the back of the worktop, pull off the lid and thrust it in front of Dana. "Look. A cake. Mum made it."

"That looks better," Dana says. "What sort of cake is it?"

"A brown one," I say, quickly putting the tin down. "What's next?"

"Err ... well, how about sewing?" Dana says. "According to your daughter's poem you're rather good at that, too."

"Yes, as a matter of fact I think I am," Mum says. "It's one of the things I'm proud of."

Proud of? A one-legged giraffe? I truly think Mum is losing her grip on reality, or at least on reality TV.

Dana says, "Emily, would you mind showing us your mum's sewing?"

I am just wondering how much public humiliation one person can handle without breakfast but I go into the living room, closely followed by Keep-Up Jim. I take a step towards the mantelpiece but just in time notice that, instead of a one-legged giraffe, there is a four-legged rat grinning at me.

"Change of plan," I yell, blocking Keep-Up Jim from coming any closer with his camera. "Look at the time. We're going to be late for Harvest Festival. Mr Meakin is very fussy about punctuality. Everybody out please." I start waving my arms and ushering people towards the door.

"Out? But we haven't finished the interview yet," Dana says. "I really want to see the sewing." She takes a step towards the mantelpiece.

"Noooo! Err . . . sewing's off. Unexpected item in the needlework area."

Dana scowls at me and turns back to the camera. "Well, it seems this interview is at an end. It's been an interesting morning, I'm sure you'll agree. And now back to the studio," she does a big false shiny smile until Keep-Up Jim says, "That's it," and then she says, "I *so* need to get back to the studio."

But if she doesn't come to the school Mrs Lovetofts will be so upset.

"Miss Devene," I say, "we would love it if you would come to our school Harvest Festival. My teacher is dying to meet you."

"A school Harvest Festival? This is not regional news, you know."

"But Mrs Lovetofts has made cushions and everything."

Dana rolls her eyes. "Look, dear, I am a very busy woman—" she starts.

Uncle Clive walks past putting his great big leather jacket on. "I'm coming, Emily," he says. "Looking forward to hearing your mum's speech. Be delighted if you would accompany me, Miss Devene." He holds out his elbow.

Dana looks at Uncle Clive, puts her arm through his and does a glossy smile. "Do you know, I think it would be a perfect end to our Mum in a Million week. Great idea, Emily," she says. "Come on, Jim. Keep up."

Yeah. Great idea, Emily. Mum, Dana, Uncle Clive, Mr Meakin and a TV camera all in the same place. What could possibly go wrong? I grab my coat and the courgette cake and follow them out.

CHAPTER TWENTY

Apple Pips and Growing Tips

Still Thursday

Fifteen minutes later, Dana, Mum, me, Chloe, Zuzanna, Uncle Clive, Gran (who says she's not missing out on the chance of a food parcel), Keep-Up Jim and the two random ladies walk into school.

Dana, Uncle Clive and the TV people go off with Mum to find Mr Meakin. Gran goes off to fight with the other old people for the best seats in the hall. Zuzanna, Chloe and I go to class, where it seems Mrs Lovetofts has already heard the good news.

"We will be going through to the hall in just a few minutes. Now I don't want everyone to get over-excited but ... Dana Devene has come to visit us. We might even be on Tee Veeeeee!" Mrs Lovetofts jumps up and down and giggles. It's not very dignified.

Everyone gasps and makes excited noises. Everyone except me because I am getting very used to being on television now. In fact, I'm probably in danger of becoming one of those worn-out child stars.

"Does everyone have their contributions to put on the Harvest Table?" Mrs Lovetofts continues when she has got her breath back. Zuzanna pulls out a box of posh cookies and I put the cake tin on the table in front of me.

"Good. So if everyone could just make sure one last time that their socks are pulled up and, Gavin, if you could just check your trousers, we are just waiting for Mr Meakin to call us through," Mrs Lovetofts says.

Everyone sits patiently except for Gross-Out and Alfie who have the combined attention span of a goldfish with ADHD. Alfie pokes two pencils up his nostrils and says, "Look, I'm a walrus." Well, actually he says, "Dook ahm ah warwus," and Gross-Out falls off his chair laughing.

"That's quite enough, boys," Mrs Lovetofts says and makes us all have another run through of "Oats and Beans and Barley Grow".

Finally, Mr Meakin taps on the door and we all file into the hall.

"Yoohoo! Emily!" Gran calls from the front row of grown-ups' chairs as I follow the rest of the children to find an uncomfortable piece of floor to sit on. She waves her handbag at me but I pretend she is just some batty old lady and ignore her. Uncle Clive is standing at the back because if he sits down no one else will be able to see anything.

Mum is sitting on the stage next to Dana and Mr Meakin. Everyone is chatting excitedly about Dana and pointing her out. I am already getting a totally worried feeling.

Mr Meakin stands up and does a little talk about how grateful we should all be that carrots were invented, and then we all have to close our eyes and pretend we are doing a silent prayer when really everyone is just thinking, *How much longer have we got to sit here?*

Then it is time to sing "Oats and Beans and Barley Grow" again. I cannot at all concentrate because I am worrying about what my mum is going to say in her talk and I get my "sows his seed" actions mixed up with my "takes his ease" actions and Zuzanna digs me with her elbow.

Then Mr Meakin says we are lucky to have Dana Devene in school and she stands up and says it's lovely to be here and gets a round of applause just for being a person.

"And now," Mr Meakin says, "Mrs Sparkes has kindly come to speak to us about Allotment Club."

Mum stands up. People start to giggle as she walks to the front of the stage in her flat cap and wellies.

"Is that really your mum, Emily Sparkes?" says Alfie Balfour.

"No," Gross-Out says, "it's Farmer Pickles," and everybody around us bursts out laughing.

I have already found out that you can't rely on the ground to swallow you up when you want it to, so I just sit on my piece of floor and feel my cheeks and ears getting hotter and hotter.

Mum stands and waits till everyone is quiet.

Then she starts to speak. "Do you know what this is?" she asks and holds up a teeny tiny speck.

"One of Alfie's headlice?" Gross-Out says.

"It's an apple pip," Mum says. "Doesn't look like much, does it? But this little pip is very clever. It has the ability to give an apple to everyone in the world." There is lots of muttering and murmuring and someone calls out, "Is it magic?"

Mum smiles. "No, not magic. Nature. If we planted this pip and looked after it, it would grow into a tree and one day that tree would have apples."

And now my ears are cooling down a bit because people have started to listen.

"Each one of those apples that grew on the tree would have lots more seeds inside. If all those seeds were allowed to grow into new trees, one day there would be enough apple trees for everyone in the world to have an apple whenever they

wanted. Nature provides us with everything we need, if we let it. All that potential from one little pip."

Some of the audience gasp. Even I'm quite interested, and I don't like apples much.

"But lots of people have forgotten this," Mum continues. "They think food comes from the supermarket. They think we have to pay big companies to produce our food and spray the earth with chemicals and kill off the tiny bugs and poison the waterways. They think that only big companies know how to feed the world. But at Juniper Road Primary, we know better. We know that a tiny seed knows how to feed the world. We know that we are tiny, too, but we can make a difference. In our Allotment Club, in our little school in Juniper Road, we're going to help our tiny seeds make a start."

There is a few seconds of silence as everyone thinks about what Mum has said and then people start clapping. Mr Meakin starts clapping, Uncle

Clive is clapping and my gran and the random ladies and all the other old people are clapping. Even Dana is clapping. And then all the children are standing up and clapping and cheering. They are all clapping and cheering my mum in her muddy jeans and old man hat.

And I don't know what it is, but I get a very funny feeling in my tummy.

Dana Devene jumps up and talks to the hall. "We are very excited to be here at the launch of Juniper Road Allotment Club. What an inspirational speech from an inspirational lady. We would like to keep in touch with the school and film your progress over the next few months, if that's OK with you, Mr Meakin."

"Absolutely," Mr Meakin says.

Chloe nudges me. "I always said that Allotment Club was a good idea. I'm signing up straight away," and she smizes enthusiastically in Dana's direction.

When the excitement has died down a bit it is time for the Harvest Festival Grand Finale where everyone gets to be publicly humiliated by the rest of the school singing about what they have put on the Harvest Table. First up is Zuzanna with a box of chocolate cookies. Mrs Whelan clunks out a tune on the piano and Mrs Lovetofts starts the singing with: "Zuzanna's brought a box of cookies, a box of cookies, a box of cookies. Zuzanna's brought a box of cookies to put on the Harvest Table."

Zuzanna stands at the front of the hall looking extremely uncomfortable until the last line when she dumps the box down on the Harvest Table and hurries back to her bit of floor.

Next up is Alfie Balfour. "What have you brought, Alfie?" asks Mrs Lovetofts.

"A tin of economy peas," Alfie says.

"Alfie's brought a tin-of-economy peas, a tin-of-economy peas, a tin-of-economy peas," Mrs Lovetofts warbles. "Come on, everyone, join in," she says. I hear my gran singing and clapping along louder than anyone else and I am very glad I didn't wave to her earlier.

There are three more people who have to suffer extreme embarrassment with "a jar of strawberry jam", "a large bunch of carrots" and "a packet of Bombay mix" before it is my turn.

I don't even feel embarrassed. Once you have faced the world's media with your mum in a scarecrow outfit, there's not much left that can faze you.

I take the cake up to the front and Mrs Lovetofts says, "What have you brought, Emily?"

"A cake," I say, and then I look at my mum and she is nodding and smiling. "A courgette cake," I say with a sigh.

Mrs Whelan bashes out the tune on the piano again, almost loud enough to drown out Chloe's cry of "Ewwwwwww!", and Mrs Lovetofts starts to sing, "Emily's brought a –"

I take the lid off the tin to show her.

"– courgette ca— aaaaah!"

Fortunately Mrs Lovetofts does not suffer a serious fainting injury because she lands on top of Mrs Whelan, who has quite a lot of personal padding. And it is also a good thing that Lemmy has eaten all the courgette cake and is too fat to jump out of the tin. I slap the lid back on again and quickly hand it to Uncle Clive, who has run up to the front to try to be a hero again.

Harvest Festival is officially abandoned because Mrs Lovetofts needs some air and none of the other teachers are any good at singing (although that's not something that ever bothers Mrs Lovetofts). We all go back to class where we have to colour in pictures of wheat and corn on the cob (which means there is a lot of arguing over yellow pencils) until Mrs Lovetofts feels well enough to think of something more educational for us to do.

Strangely, Mrs Lovetofts doesn't say anything to me about Lemmy being in the cake tin. Perhaps she thinks she imagined him – teachers can get very stressed about school celebrations.

At lunch time I go to see if Mum is still around. She is in the corridor putting up another Allotment Club poster. She has written "Allotment Club: Grand Re-launch Tomorrow Lunchtime. Key Stage Two Only" in big black letters across the top. There is already a queue of people waiting to sign it. I think I'll let them get on with it this time.

"That was a good speech, Mum," I say and she looks very pleased. "Although it would have been better if you'd worn a dress," I add. "Where's Uncle Clive?"

"He went. Daisy came to pick him up. Apparently she was watching TV this morning and saw him being a hero with Dana and she's considering forgiving him for the aromatherapy oil incident."

I notice Mum's crossed her fingers.

Dana and Keep-Up Jim seem to have spent a useful morning drinking coffee and eating biscuits in the staff room and are getting ready to go back to TV land.

"Thank you for showing us your interesting lifestyle choices," Dana says to Mum. "Although it's a pity we didn't get to see your sewing."

"Follow me," Mum says and heads out of the door and across the school field. Dana and Keep-Up Jim walk out behind her. I don't know what she's up to but I think I'd better tag along too.

Dana tiptoes across the field behind Mum, trying not to let her high heels sink into the mud. "I'm beginning to see why you like your wellies so much," she says. "Come on, Jim. Keep up."

Mum points to the very muddy allotment patch. "Needs a lot of work yet," she says, "but a couple of days ago I made a start and put in some broad beans for next year. That's the sort of sowing I'm good at."

"Ha ha," Dana laughs. "Now that is definitely a useful skill."

And I suddenly have that very strange feeling again but this time I know what it is. I am feeling very proud of my mum.

We all go in to see Mrs Lovetofts who is waiting to get Dana's opinion on the classroom cushions. She is so excited when Dana says they are "ravishingly retro" that I am worried she might faint again. Chloe does a lot of smizing and gets everyone's autograph including Keep-Up Jim and the two random ladies and then it is time for Dana to go back to TV land. "Don't forget to watch in the morning when we give out the prizes," Dana says, "and we'll definitely be back to see how those broad beans are coming on."

A big van with "Dana Devene: Domestic Queen" in curly writing down the side pulls up outside and Dana and Keep-Up Jim get in.

It is only when they are pulling away that I notice the two random ladies are still there.

"Aren't you going with them?" I ask.

"Oh no," says one of them. "We were only passing by this morning, and just wondered what the excitement was all about."

CHAPTER TWENTY-ONE

Mum in a Million

Friday

I am very glad this is the last morning I have to get up early to watch breakfast TV. This has been the most tiring week of my life. I am eating my Coco-Crispies and it is taking most of my last bit of energy. Mum is drinking tea in her old dressing gown and Gran has come round especially early and is squashed in between us on the sofa. We are all waiting to see the results of the Mum in a Million competition.

Dad had to go to work early but he said he already knows that Mum is a Mum in a Million anyway so he doesn't need to see the results. Mum says he's only saying that because he doesn't want her to leave him in charge of Clover again.

"You know, I haven't really got a hope of winning," Mum says. "They want someone who can cook and sew and although I did my best I think maybe I'm better at other things."

Dana Devene appears and she looks a bit tired herself. I suppose she's had a pretty busy week too. "Welcome, everyone. I'm sure you're all dying to know the final results of our Mum in a Million competition. We've met three very different but very talented ladies this week. It was a difficult decision but without further ado we've decided the best all-round mum and homemaker, who will win the top prize, is ..."

I can't cross my fingers because I am holding my Coco-Crispies so I cross my toes and squeeze my eyes shut.

"Janine!" Dana says.

Janine. Nooooo. I feel so disappointed. It's silly because I know my mum wasn't the sort of person they were looking for but she did try hard and I was so proud of her yesterday.

"What?" Gran says, jumping up and spilling her tea. "Janine? All she did was make a load of old curtains and things. Fix! Fix!" she shouts at the TV. "It's Brenda Belter all over again."

"Oh well, that's that," Mum says, picking up the remote to turn off the TV. "I never thought there was any chance. And I don't want a makeover anyway, but I'm sorry you didn't get your trip to London."

"Don't worry, Mum," I say. "Anyway, like Bella says, being able to cook and sew doesn't make you a good mum, anyone can learn that. There are loads more important things, like caring about the world and having interesting ideas. You are definitely the best at that."

Mum gives me a big hug, a Mum in a Million hug.

"Wait," Gran says. "Listen."

"However," Dana continues, "we would like to give a special mention to Eco-Mum Amanda Sparkes. I'm sure any of you who watched the show yesterday morning will agree that she has a somewhat ... *individual* take on cooking and interior decorating," she says with a smile. "However, we would like you to see this moving speech she gave at her daughter's school, which we filmed later."

The picture cuts to my mum, standing on the school stage, holding up an apple pip. And even though she is in front of the whole world in her flat cap and wellies, this time I don't feel embarrassed one bit.

"We will be following the progress of Juniper

Road Primary and their lovely Allotment Club over the coming months," says Dana. "And now back to our Mum in a Million, Janine . . ."

Mum stands up and clicks off the TV. "We're going to have to make a good job of this allotment now," she says. "Don't forget your wellies today, Em."

At lunchtime, Allotment Club is super popular. Everyone has brought in their wellies and quite a few have got poodles or ladybirds on after all. Chloe says she has a rare allergy to wellies and therefore can't get involved with the muddy bit, but she said she's quite happy to be my mum's personal assistant and handle any TV or publicity issues that crop up.

"Everyone ready to make Juniper Road Primary start changing the world?" Mum says.

"Yes!" everyone shouts back.

"Let's get on with it then!"

We work very hard all lunchtime and at the end it looks . . . mostly like a weedy patch of mud still.

"Good work, everyone," Mum says. "Thank you for your help, see you all next week."

Everyone has had loads of fun and can't stop chattering about what we are going to grow for next year.

"Sweetcorn," says Joshua.

"Petit pois," says Babette.

"Ewww," Chloe says. "Can't we just grow peas?"

I walk back across the field with Mum. "It was fun today, Mum," I say. "Everyone's excited about what we're going to grow."

Mum sighs. "I know. We really could do with some proper equipment though. If we're going to make any real progress, we're not going to do it with a few old sandpit spades and a wheelbarrow with a flat tyre." She looks at her watch. "Goodness, is that the time already? I've got to get back. Gran's dropping Clover off in ten minutes. She's starting her Criminology class this afternoon."

CHAPTER TWENTY-TWO

Room for Improvement

Still Friday

My mum has gone viral! Chloe messaged me on the way home from school in her capacity as Publicity Manager:

OM actual G. Your Mum is on YouTube!!!!!

Apparently Keep-Up Jim put the video online this afternoon and it has had 50,000 hits already. ("Going viral" and "getting hits" all sounds quite unpleasant. I think the Internet should make up some better ways of putting it. I might do that when I have time.)

Everyone is calling her the Apple Pip Woman. Bella messaged me to say they have even seen her in Wales.

The phone is ringing non-stop with people asking Mum to come and speak at their school or do an interview for their magazine (and also Mr Bevan-at-number-thirty-seven saying his shower's leaking again).

But the best thing is, Seeds 'n' Weeds, the garden centre near school, is going to donate a whole load of equipment. Spades, forks, plants and even a greenhouse!

"So much better than a makeover," Mum says. "It's an allotment makeover!"

Gran has come round to celebrate. She has

bought my mum a pair of green wellies (thank you, Gran) and a fleece from Marks & Spencer.

And Uncle Clive has come round too. To collect his things! Daisy has forgiven him. "She thought I was very brave," he says, carrying his rucksack out to the hall. "She didn't think much of Dana, though. Thanks for the loan of the room, Emily. You can have it back now."

"Great!" I say, heading for the stairs.

"Hang on, Emily," Mum says. "I'll come up with you. It probably needs a bit of tidying up."

I am so relieved to get my room back. I love Clover and she is fun to play with but not at three in the morning when you have to get up for school, and sleeping on a camp bed is rubbish if you're not on actual holiday. I push open the door to my room, but something has happened. It is not my room. There is no Taylor Swift with Pudsey ears, there is no faded pink paint or chocolate milkshake stain on the carpet. There are pale purple walls

267

and a raspberry pink rug. There is a purple and lilac duvet cover and pretty cushions on the bed. There are matching curtains and two beanbags in the corner, next to the mended bookshelves and mended wardrobe. There is even a new desk with a lamp and Wavey Cat sitting on it. I can't take it all in.

I turn round to find Mum, Clover and Uncle Clive behind me, all grinning.

"We had a little bit of a tidy up," Mum says.

"But when? How?" I say, sounding like Mrs Lovetofts in creative writing mode again.

"Well, Uncle Clive has been spending a lot of time in his room," Mum laughs. "Mostly with a paintbrush."

"And your mum has been spending a lot of time in the shed," Uncle Clive says.

"But what have you been doing in the shed?"

"Sewing curtains and cushions," Mum says. "I've

learned quite a lot from watching Dana, you know. Look I even re-covered your headboard with some fabric and a staple gun."

"But if you'd shown Dana all this yesterday, you might have won."

"I wasn't really finished," Mum says, "and anyway, I didn't want to spoil your surprise."

"It's all great," I say.

"We gave Wavey Cat pride of place," Mum says, flicking his paw. "I found a note that you wrote about how you couldn't do without him; it was very sweet."

"That was supposed to be homework," I say.

"I've still got it if you want to hand it in," Mum says.

"Don't worry," I say. "I ... err ... handed something else in."

I can't stop looking around my room. It is fantastic, it is brilliant. It is better than any bedroom in the world. I have run out of words.

"Thank you," I say, giving Mum a big hug and Uncle Clive a sort of head butt in the chest.

"You're welcome," Uncle Clive says. "Thanks for the loan of the room. And all the other help *rat* you gave me." He chuckles and heads off downstairs, leaving Mum looking confused. "Bye, Emily," he calls. "Bye, Flora."

"Clover!" we call after him.

"Sorry," he says and we hear the front door slam.

"This room is great, Mum," I say. "In fact, you are definitely a Mum in a Million!"

"Definitely," Mum says.

"I've got one question, though," I say.

"Yes?"

"Is it shabby chic or tasteful?"

ACKNOWLEDGEMENTS

With thanks to my fab editor Kate, and all at Hachette Children's Group, especially Becca, Caitlin and Louise. More thanks to Gemma and Team Cooper for being top supporters. Love and thanks to Dali, Edie and Louis for putting up with a mum who lives in a book, and to Laura and Mick and my mum who also wears wellies.

ABOUT THE AUTHOR

Ruth Fitzgerald was born in Bridgend, South Wales. She grew up in a happy, big, noisy family with far too many brothers.

When she was six years old she wrote her first story, "Mitzi the Mole Gets Married", and *immediately* announced she wanted to be a writer. Her teacher *immediately* advised her that writing was a hobby and she needed to get a proper job. Since then she has tried twenty-three proper jobs but really the only thing she likes doing is writing.

Ruth lives in Suffolk with her family, one very small dog and five chickens. They are all very supportive of her writing, although the chickens don't say a lot.

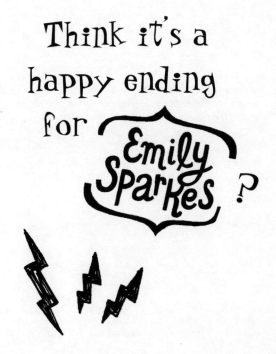

Think again...

For Emily Sparkes news, reviews

and totally awesome downloads

visit www.ruthfitzgerald.co.uk